12 Days of Smutmas

HOLIDAY SHORT STORIES

DANA LEEANN

ONE MORE CHAPTER PUBLISHING LLC

Content & Copyright

First Edition November 2023

Cover by Dana LeeAnn
Edited by Rocky Calvo with Rocky Calvo Edits
Published by One More Chapter Publishing LLC

Inquiries: **danaleeannauthor@gmail.com**

Trigger Warnings

**YOUR MENTAL HEALTH MATTERS.
READ THIS PAGE IN ITS ENTIRETY.**

This book contains(but not limited to) content depicting **sexual content, dark themes, knife play, taboo themes including religion, degradation, explicit sexual content, explicit language, bondage, BDSM, punishment, age gap, whipping, breath play/choking, food play, mention of alcoholism, mention of drug addition, anal, snow play, public sex, mention of murder, double penetration, sex without a condom, blood, blood play**

This book is not intended for readers under the age of 18. Read with caution. Your mental health matters.

The book you are about to read is dark, wild, and not recommended for all readers. Read through the trigger warnings once more, then decide if you should continue on with this book.

If you find a trigger I haven't listed, please reach out through email and let me know. I've done my best to get them all, but it's possible some have slipped through the cracks with twelve different stories.

Email: danaleeannauthor@gmail.com

FINAL TRIGGER WARNING:

Sexual content, dark themes, knife play, taboo themes including religion, degradation, explicit sexual content, explicit language, bondage, BDSM, punishment, age gap, whipping, breath play/choking, food play, mention of alcoholism, mention of drug addition, anal, snow play, public sex, mention of murder, double penetration, sex without a condom, blood, blood play

12 Days of Smutmas

Twelve holiday-themed short stories filled with spice and everything nice. Each story is unique, containing its own variety of characters and plots. Read one short story a day for twelve days to complete 12 Days of Smutmas.

Day One: Santa's Helper

Day Two: Big Red Bow

Dat Three: Candy Cane Core

Day Four: Working the North Pole

Day Five: Sugarplum Party

Day Six: Gingerbread Daddy

Day Seven: Mistletoe Manor

Day Eight: Snow Play

Day Nine: Whipped by Winters

Day Ten: The Naughty Elf

Day Eleven: Garland Gag

Day Twelve: On Donner, On Vixen

Merry Smutmas, you filthy hoe hoe hoes.

I hope Santa stuffs your stocking with his load.

Author's Note

12 Days of Smutmas is meant to be ***fun.*** It's not meant to be serious, or deep, or full of plot. The majority of these stories include the main characters meeting for the first time, then having wild and crazy sex *very* soon after. If this doesn't sound ***fun*** to you, then this probably isn't meant for you. I say this in the least offensive way possible because I want you to *enjoy* the books you consume.

The stories within this collection are not meant to be realistic. This is a work of smutty fiction, and it will certainly read that way. Some stories are on the sweeter side, while others are dark and dirty.

If this sounds like the book for you, I'm so excited for you to get your eyes on it. Reach out and let me know if you love it as much as I do. I live for connecting with my readers. I appreciate each and every one of you.

Santa's Helper

ALYSSA & SANTA

"So, Alyssa, what did you think of today's event?" Santa asks as the last child exits the privately reserved room with his parents, his voice deep.

Biting my lip, I'm unsure how to respond. The truth is, I've been overwhelmed by the sheer amount of children begging Santa for what they wanted for Christmas. When I took the job filling in for Suze last minute, I didn't realize there would be hundreds of needy children wrapped around the shopping mall, all waiting for their turn to sit on Santa's lap. Suzy is sick today and asked me to take her place at Santa's side.

Most of the children were on the nice list, but there was a rather large handful of those on the naughty list. We could spot the naughty children from a mile away, and

Santa said there were more this year than usual. He blames the overuse of electronics and lack of fresh air, but I'm more convinced it's red food dye and insufficient nutrients.

Santa sees the hesitation written all over my face and speaks again. "It's okay, Alyssa. I know it was a lot to take in on your first day, but I'm glad you were here. You did great."

I smile, relieved to hear the praise coming from Santa's lips. Nodding, I can feel my cheeks flush with warmth. I hadn't expected Santa to notice me. I'm nothing more than a helper elf, and I'm here to direct the flow of children while ensuring the Christmas chaos stays to a minimum.

Patting my shoulder, Santa's large, firm hands make me blush even more. He seems to take note of my reaction and grins accordingly, his bright eyes twinkling against the fluorescent mall lights. This Santa is younger than the Santas in previous generations. He's in his mid-forties, and he hasn't filled out the suit in the same way the others have. The Santa gene made his hair grey at an early age, but it makes him look like more of a fine wine.

A *silver fox,* if you will.

Did I mention he's single?

This Santa is strong. He's toned. *Fit.* We have to stuff his suit with stuffing to make him look more filled out; otherwise, children question him and stop believing.

Santa leans back in his oversized chair, watching me as he says, "It's about time to head home, but I think it'd be nice to take a few minutes to relax before we head for the sleigh." There's a strange look in his eye. "Would you like to join me?"

I glance at him, confused. "You mean, here? In the mall?"

With a serious face, Santa nods. "Yes. I think it would be nice to get to know one another on a *deeper* level. What do you say?"

Pausing, I'm unsure what to do. I *do* want to spend more time with Santa, but I'm not sure if it's appropriate. Especially here, in the shopping mall. The only thing separating us from the public is a set of glass doors with its hours etched into the glass. Anyone could ignore the time and walk in.

Then again, I don't want to make my first day working with Santa awkward by turning him down, and I *am* attracted to him. Alone time with him would be nice. Perhaps I could be the next Mrs. Claus...

"Yes, I would love to join you," I say.

His face lights up with a broad grin, and he motions for me to sit on his lap. The slap of his hand against his thigh sends shivers down my spine, and I'm feeling unexpectedly aroused.

"You... You want me to sit on your lap?" I raise a brow to Santa, trying to get a more accurate read on him.

He's watching me intently through icy blue eyes. "Yes," he growls, low and deep, so quietly I almost don't hear him.

Nodding, I cross the few feet of open space between us before carefully lowering myself onto his lap, my legs dangling over the side of his thighs.

His hands immediately find my hips, steading me as I settle in. Our eyes meet, and my breath catches in my throat. His eyes are glowing as he studies my face up close, and I find myself lost in a trance.

He chuckles, seeming to know what I'm thinking. His hands move to my waist, gently caressing the skin beneath my uniform. I gasp softly as a wave of electricity jolts through me. His hands continue to move over my body, only pausing to read my face to make sure it's okay to keep going, and a wet heat begins to build between my thighs. My breath quickens and my heart begins to race as Santa's gentle hands explore my body.

This was... *unexpected.*

But I'm loving it. I've watched Santa from a distance from the moment he took over, and just like every other worker elf, I dreamed of being in the running for the future Mrs. Claus... but that's all it was.

A dream.

And yet, here I am, seated in Santa's lap with his hardening cock pressing against my backside.

He stops, locking his eyes with mine. His gaze is so intense I feel my heart skip a beat. My body tenses as he removes his hands from my waist and plants them firmly on my ass.

His voice is even deeper than before, almost throaty, and he's so still as he says, "It seems as though you've been a naughty girl today."

I blush, wanting to move away from him as my cheeks burn with embarrassment, but I'm frozen in time as his gaze holds me. I'd blame his magic or mistletoe, but that's not what's going on here. This is pure unbridled lust radiating between us.

"Are you okay with this?" he asks as his thumb strokes my ass.

Nodding, I shift into his lap, purposely grinding myself against his erect cock. "Yes."

"I want you bent over my knee," Santa snaps. "Naughty girls as pretty as you deserve to be spanked."

"What did I do, Santa?" I ask, not completely sure if he's roleplaying or if I actually did something wrong.

A sly smirk slides across his face and his eyes darken as he watches me. "You aren't already on your knees begging for my cock, Alyssa. That's a *very* naughty girl." His grip tightens around my ass. "If you don't want coal for Christmas, I suggest you start behaving."

Stunned, I'm wide-eyed and dazed. My stomach tightens as he lightly slaps my ass, encouraging me to bend myself over his knee. I jump off his lap, then lower myself over his knee, bracing myself against his thighs.

Taking his time, Santa rolls his palm flatly against my ass, running in circular motions. His touch is firm, and I know he's not going to be nice. He hikes my skirt up to my stomach, exposing my bare ass to him.

I knew there would be a day where going commando would pay off, and this is it. Smiling to myself, I grin widely as he realizes I'm not wearing any panties.

"A very, *very* naughty girl, Alyssa," Santa repeats as his eyes roam my exposed flesh.

His fingers slide between my folds, rubbing up and down against my pussy as a satisfied moan slips through his lips. His fingers glide through my arousal with ease, and I know I'm already ready for him.

Raising his hand above his head, Santa brings it down, striking my skin with a thunderous crack that rings out through the entire mall, and I find myself glancing toward the doors to make sure no one outside heard it. His hand climbs through the air again, bringing his hand down a second time with just as much force as the first.

I cry out, painful pleasure ripping through me as my arousal spikes.

"I want to be a good girl, Santa," I pant through shallow breaths. "How can I be good for you?" I whimper in a playful voice.

Stroking his long beard, Santa thinks for a moment while I'm bent over his knee.

Eventually, he nods, coming to a conclusion. "I will consider moving you to my nice list if you ride my cock."

Excitement tingles through me, and I nearly scramble to my feet, but I hold it together. If I want to play the long game of becoming Mrs. Claus, I'll need to play it cool.

"I want to be good for you, Santa," I purr as I remove myself from his lap, staring at the hard bulge poking out of his red suit. "I want to make you feel good after a long day at work."

"Hop on," Santa whispers through gritted teeth as he points at his dick, and I can tell he's trying to hold it together just as much as I am.

"With pleasure," I lightly bow with my bottom lip sucked between my teeth.

Santa wiggles his pants down just low enough to let his cock spring free, and my mouth waters at the glorious sight. Hiking my skirt up higher to give my hips a full range of motion, I climb back into his lap, this time facing him.

With his thick cock in my hand, I don't break eye contact with him as I lower myself onto him, letting him sink deep into my core.

"Mmm," I moan as his dick plunges all the way into me.

I still myself when he's fully inside me, savoring the fullness of his dick. My pussy clenches around him, and he grips my hips as I begin to move my body up and down, gliding over him.

My voice is shallow as I breathe, "Am I a good girl yet, Santa?"

"You're getting closer, but you're not there yet," he groans as he confirms my suspicions.

"If I ride your cock every day, will it keep me at the top of the nice list?"

"Fuck yes," he hisses as I pick up the pace, grinding myself against him. "You'll put yourself in first place with that attitude."

Music to my ears.

I can already taste my new title: Mrs. Claus.

Bracing my hands against his chest, I lean into him as I move, bouncing up and down while he holds my hips, slamming me down hard on his cock.

I cry out with pleasure, moaning through each delicious rise and fall of my hips.

"You're such a good fucking girl," he grunts as he slams me down harder, reaching his climax and emptying his seed inside of me.

I come with him, unraveling as I explode. My hips are rhythmic as we fuck through our orgasms, drawing them out as long as we can before coming down from the high. I slow, stilling my body over him before rising and letting his soft dick fall out of me.

Pleased with my work, I toss Santa one of the disposable towels we use for crying parents and children. He cleans himself up, then watches me as I fix my skirt. His cum is leaking out of me, dripping down my inner thighs, but I leave it as a reminder of how lucky I am to fuck Santa.

I'll fuck my way to the top of his list, and I'll enjoy every second of it.

Big Red Bow

JESS & ZACH

I'm a creature of anticipation. I thrive in the moments when time slows down and I'm forced to wait, my heart thumping with the excitement of what's to come. I've been waiting all day for my boyfriend, Zach, to come home from his corporate office job. Before he left for work this morning, he said my Christmas present would be ready by the time he got home.

The sun is fading over the horizon, and I can feel my anticipation reaching a high point.

I wanted to be ready for anything the night would have in store for me, but my head has been foggy, so I've been lying in bed all day. There's a thin white sheet draped over my body and I've got a fully charged vibrator in my hand.

Slowly, I slip the vibrator between my legs, feeling my sensitive skin come to life with each hum of the device. If Zach was here, he'd fuck me with his massive cock while I hold this vibrator to my clit, but he's not here, so I'll have to be creative.

Turning onto my stomach, I arch my back, thrusting my ass into the air and spreading my legs wide while holding the vibrator to my clit. I moan loudly, crying out as the pleasure rolls through me. Rolling it in firm, circular motions, I'm able to bring my orgasm to the surface within seconds, and I'm convulsing around the vibrator. My body quivers and shakes as I whimper, riding out the orgasm and grinding myself harder into the vibrator.

My orgasm reaches its peak, then I come down from the high. That's the fourth orgasm I've given myself today, and if Zach doesn't get home soon I'll do it again to keep my head clear.

Through the crack in my bedroom door, I hear the sound of a key unlocking the front door. Our home security system beeps, announcing his entrance. My heart rate spikes with excitement knowing he's home.

Throwing the vibrator in the drawer of my nightstand, I jump out of bed, grabbing a fluffy red robe as I race out the door, nearly stumbling to get to him. As I open the door, I imagine all the things Zach could be surprising me with.

He's rich as fuck, and he's not one to skimp out on my gifts. With it being so close to Christmas, I know it's going to be big. He's given me everything from fine jewelry to luxurious European vacations.

I race down the hall, meeting Zach at the front entrance. He's dressed in his Friday casual attire: light grey slacks and a white fitted button-up shirt.

"Hey, beautiful," he smiles when he sees me, setting down his briefcase.

"Hey," I say as he wraps me in his arms.

Breathing in his musky cedarwood scent, I want this moment to last forever. His hands lightly graze my skin, igniting a fire deep within my core. I yearn for more, and in my state of lust, I nearly forget that only moments before, I was pleasuring myself with my vibrator instead of his dick.

It's been a long week. Zach has all the money a girl could need and more, but I'm an independent woman and I've still got a job. I've been looking forward to the weekend with Zach. This week has been particularly difficult, and I'm ready for something different, but adulting doesn't allow me to just quit my job.

Breaking our hug, Zach takes a step back, eyeing me up and down in my robe. He sucks his lower lip between his bottom teeth as his eyes travel my body, and I can see the hunger in his eyes. Shaking his head subtly, Zach pulls himself back into reality.

“Come outside. I’ve got a surprise for you,” he grins.

Taking his hand, I follow Zach outside. The breeze is warm and the sun is shining. We round the corner, stepping into the open as the driveway expands before us.

I gasp and my jaw drops as a brand new, stunning, and pearly white Range Rover comes into view. There’s a giant red bow perched atop the hood, and I realize it’s mine.

“You didn’t!” I scream, drawing the attention of neighbors.

The car sparkles in the sunlight and the chrome accents gleam brightly.

Turning to Zach, my billionaire boyfriend, I find his eyes twinkling with mischievousness, and I can tell he’s up to something.

I raise my brow to him, and question, “What?”

He takes me by the hand, slowly leading me around the car, pointing out all of its features, all while talking in his low, commanding voice.

The voice that makes me so fucking *wet* for him.

He speaks of the car's power, of its luxury, and of its speed. It's a dream come true. I've wanted a white Range Rover for as long as I can remember, and he made it a reality.

When he's finished showing me everything there is to know about the car, Zach moves toward the hood of the car, reaching for the big red bow. He unties it slowly, letting the red ribbon curl around his hands before taking my arms and tying them together tightly behind my back.

I don't fight him as he secures the bow. The fabric of the ribbon is tight around my wrists, and I can feel a thrill of excitement running through me. Looking into Zach's eyes, he's smiling down at me with a familiar hunger.

He's as powerful as the car he bought me, and as I stare into his eyes, I can feel the power he has over me. My arousal is instant, and I cross my legs as my clit begins to pulse.

Zach leans in, kissing me gently on my lips. His kiss feels like a promise, sending electric sparks through my body as he deepens it, drawing me closer to him. My robe slips open, exposing one of my breasts to the warm sunshine.

Wide-eyed, I reach to cover myself, but I'm quickly reminded my hands are securely tied behind my back.

A wicked smirk spreads across Zach's lips, and that's when I realize this is exactly what he wants. I'm his to do with as he pleases, to take my body however he wants, whenever he wants. He steps closer, close enough to feel the warmth of his body against mine, and I watch him inhale my scent.

He wants me.

He *needs* me.

Breaking the silence again, he asks, "What do you think of your present?"

I hesitate, unsure of the game he's playing. "It's beautiful," I say breathlessly.

"Good," he smirks, his voice low and deep. He clicks a button on the key fob, and the car roars to life, the engine purring. "Let's go for a ride."

"Now?" I ask, glancing down at his hardening dick, sucking my lip between my teeth.

"I want to take *you* for a ride, Jess."

Realization dawns on me, and I suddenly understand what he means. Zach's fingers trace the shape of my face before drifting lower, to the opening of my robe. He opens it wider, exposing both of my breasts. The robe is tied just below my breasts, and his hand dips lower. Pulling on the string before I can comprehend what he's doing, he lets the robe fall wide open.

I yelp in surprise as he grabs me around the waist, his hands possessive and strong. Melting into his embrace, I can feel his heart racing against mine. Turning my body around, Zach slams me onto the hood of the car.

Gasping as he presses himself into me, my eyes flutter closed while he nibbles down my neck, his hands stroking my body as I shiver in delight. His hands move lower, fingertips grazing over my curves and exploring my body. A soft moan escapes my lips as he teases my nipples, sending sparks of pleasure throughout my entire body.

He continues lower, and I inhale sharply as he slides his hand between my legs. My body quivers as he touches my pussy, heating my insides as he begins rubbing between my folds. His fingers move expertly against my most sensitive parts, teasing and stroking until I can't take it anymore.

I cry out with pleasure as he dips a finger inside of me, the sensation sending shockwaves through my body. He begins fingering me harder, slamming my tied body against the hood of my new car. My wet pussy stretches to fit him as he slips a second finger inside of me.

Hiking my right leg up on the car, he presses into me harder, and my clit rubs against the pearly metallic finish as he thrusts his fingers in and out of me. The purr of the engine feels exactly like my vibrator, and I moan so loudly I'm sure the neighbors are watching, but I don't care.

We've never cared.

My orgasm builds so quickly as he drives me toward the edge, drawing my pleasure out one delicious stroke at a time. Zach pulls my hair, forcing my head back as he fucks me with his fingers.

"Fuck, Zach." I'm nearly screaming. "I'm going to come."

"Come for me, baby," he moans against my neck.

And I do, so fucking hard. I scream his name as my pussy clamps down on his thick fingers, and my stomach tightens against the car. My orgasm rips through me and I can barely breathe as I come down from the high.

I turn around to face Zach, and he's already freeing his dick from his pants. Without hesitation, I drop to my knees, my hands still securely tied behind my back. My lips part for him as he lines his cock up to my face. He slides it past the entrance of my mouth, and I flatten my tongue against him. Bobbing my head, I slurp him down inch by inch, letting him in deeper and deeper until he's pressing against the back of my throat. The urge to gag is strong, so strong I nearly pull back, but I press on, drinking him down until he grabs the back of my head.

Zach holds onto my hair while he fucks my mouth. Saliva seeps from the sides of my mouth.

Messy and wet, just how he *loves* it.

Thrusting to the back of my throat, Zach holds his cock there to cut off my breathing, and he waits until the last second to withdraw himself from my mouth.

"Stand up," he orders, pulling on my arm as I rise to my feet. He turns me to lean me over the car again, but instead of fucking me with his fingers, he slams his dick inside of me.

Raw and wet, I take him as deep as he can thrust. We're both moaning and crying out in pleasure as he fucks me from behind. As he gives me a ride on his cock.

I push against him, meeting each of his thrusts, and it's like we're in a trance, moving as one to reach our orgasms. The pleasure is overwhelming, and he's driving me dangerously close to the edge.

Another thrust and my pleasure crests. I scream out in pleasure, and I notice the neighbors next door are standing in their driveway, silently watching us. I think they secretly like it, and it only encourages me to be louder.

This isn't anything they haven't seen from us before, so I might as well put on a show.

Zach continually slams in and out of me as quickly as he can, ramping up the pace as he nears his climax.

"Come with me," I encourage him, begging him to join me in the euphoric high of our orgasms.

A loud grunt leaves Zach as he pounds my pussy, and I know he's coming. My pussy clamps down around his dick, and I come with him. I don't take my eyes off the neighbor as he watches, and he doesn't look away. He returns my stare with a challenge of his own, and I have a feeling this will be our new little game.

Candy Cane Core

RHETT & HOLLY

WRITTEN BY MELISSA MCSHERRY

The way Holly sucks my dick is fucking perfection. The church choir chants "O Holy Night" loudly in the other room, and what a holy night it's turned out to be.

For me, anyway.

I thought being sent to spend Christmas Eve in my least favorite church in New York would be less... eventful. Sure, I was eager to get eyes on Jose Demarko, leader of the Don Leon Cartel for the first time since he went dark two years ago, but never did I think our first sighting would be at a damn midnight Mass.

He didn't stay long. Halfway through, he got what appeared to be an urgent phone call and left without exchanging goodbyes with family. I wanted to follow him. I *knew* it was an essential part of my plan to draw him away from his people, especially after how many years he's spent in hiding.

I'm not God's favorite, so even though it's Christmas Eve, he likes to fuck shit up for me.

There was no way I could've followed him out without blowing my cover. Even with a distraction as brilliant as a church full of family, he has this place packed with his men, all undercover and patiently waiting for a chance to strike down the first threat that comes along. Thanks to my unmatched ability to think ahead, I managed to get a tracker on the back bumper of his blacked-out SUV as I passed by on my way in, which allowed me to sit back and relax while he gets a head start, and it won't flag his men to my presence.

I knew if I came into the church looking the way I do, covered in ink and dark leather, I'd quickly attract unwanted attention. Thankfully, while planting my tracker on Jose's SUV, I spotted a *very* drunk, *very* tweaked-out Santa just down the block. His pathetic attempts at handing out candy canes to unsuspecting juveniles made me nauseous, and it wasn't hard to convince him to follow me to the back of an abandoned building where there was a lack of both cameras and witnesses.

I threw his costume over my clothing after dumping his body in the dumpster out back and strolled back down the street and into Mass, and no one seemed to know any different. No one would suspect Santa.

Except for Holly, that is.

My head falls back against the wood panel wall as a moan slips from my lips. Every run of her tongue down my shaft, every scrape of her teeth against the barbells of my piercings... it's pure and utter torture– in all the good ways. She fucking worships my dick with that unholy mouth of hers, like I am her preacher and she's in dire need of a baptism. Fisting her hair in my hand, I shove her face down, forcing myself to the back of her throat. Her eyes widen, but not with fear.

No, Holly is too much of a filthy little slut for fear.

She fucking gets off on this shit.

She's not afraid to choke or gag on my dick. All she cares about is swallowing my load like it's her Communion bread, and she takes every fucking drop.

Thank God she does because it's the only thing that keeps me coming back. Don't get me wrong, she's hot as fuck and her tits were sculpted by Jesus Christ himself, but she's not my type.

Not by a long shot.

She's rich, snobby, and treats everyone around her like the shit that seeps from her gaping asshole. Behind closed doors, though, where her preacher daddy can't see her, she's a fucking freak. Just freaky enough to make me forget how much I fucking *loathe* her existence.

When my balls are smacking against her full lips, I could care less how much I hate her.

Shoving myself to the back of her throat again, I force her head down on my cock until she gags, then pull myself out. She stares up at me with pleading eyes, her mascara ruined and running down her pretty little face. Her lips are swollen and red from sucking me off, and I watch as she runs her tongue out across them before pulling her bottom lip into her mouth.

"Get up," I command her, and like the good little slut she is, she obeys, quickly pushing herself off her knees and to her feet. I tower over her petite frame as I guide her further into the preacher's office. Once inside, I shove her until she falls backward into a chair behind the desk.

Her God-loving daddy's desk.

Keeping my eyes locked with hers, I lower myself between her legs and allow myself a moment to take in how fucking perfect she looks tonight. The low-cut black sequin dress hugs every curve of her body like it was made for her, leaving nothing to the imagination. I push the lower part of her dress up her thighs until her core is revealed to me.

Fuck.

She's soaked right through her white cotton panties.

"Look how wet you are. Such a filthy little whore, aren't you, Holly?" I whisper. "You like sucking my cock, don't you?"

"Yes," she mutters through shallow breaths as I run my fingers over her drenched panties.

"Good girl," I say, standing to full height with my hands braced against my hips. "Now, it's Christmas Eve, and you haven't given me a gift yet. You're a very naughty girl."

"But I just sucked your-" She stops mid-sentence as I slap her mouth with my fingertips.

"You willingly get on your knees for me anytime I ask, Holly. That hardly counts as a Christmas gift. So tonight, you're going to give me something else," I reply, pulling her panties to the side as I circle evidence of arousal around her clit.

Her pussy glistens in the white light of the office, and although I've never eaten her out, watching my fingers spread her juices around has me wanting to taste how sweet her perfect little cunt is before I ruin it.

After all, Christmas is the season for giving, right?

Perhaps by gifting Holly here with as many orgasms as she can handle, our Lord and Savior will wash away some of my sins. I quietly chuckle to myself. Who the fuck am I kidding? My sins are etched into my flesh, sewn into my very soul. There's no washing them away. If anything, fucking the preacher's daughter is simply adding to them, but that's what makes it exciting. Thrilling.

"Wh-what do you want? I'll do anything. Please."

Hearing a woman beg to worship my cock has got to be the best fucking sound to ever meet my ears. The chair's wheels roll, knocking the chair into her daddy's desk, drawing my attention to a jumbo candy cane that sits on a thick stack of papers. My cock twitches as an idea forms in my mind. I quickly grab it off the desk, sending sheets of paper to the carpeted floor.

She eyes me, confused and watching me as I tear at the thin plastic wrapped around the fat candy with my teeth.

"What are you going to do?" she whimpers.

"Well, Holly. Santa is going to do whatever he wants with you and your pretty little pussy, and you're going to enjoy it. *That* is my gift. Are we clear?"

"Yes," she whispers, nodding as her eyes trail me. I run the end of the peppermint candy cane through the slick folds of her pussy, coating it in her arousal as her head falls back against the chair. I pause until her heated gaze snaps to mine.

"Yes, what?"

"Yes, Santa," she cries out.

A coy smile forms on my lips as I bring the thick candy back to her pussy, continuing to slide it around her tight little hole, teasing her. She squirms in her daddy's squeaky office chair as the candy's hard tip circles her swollen clit.

"That's a good girl. You like the way Santa's candy feels, don't you?"

She's such a needy little slut, and although all she's ever done is suck me dry, I'm kicking it up a notch tonight. Tonight, while her daddy is in the other room praising the Lord and Savior, I'll have his precious daughter bent over his desk, praising me and my cock as I fuck her into the holiday spirit.

Without warning, I slide the candy cane in and out of her pussy. Precum beads on the tip of my cock as I watch her heated core swallow the sweet candy stick. Her back arches off the chair as she gasps at the unexpected assault.

She's fucking *loving* this.

"This is what happens when you make Santa's naughty list, Holly. You get teased and treated like the little slut you are."

Her moans echo around the small office, mingling with the chanting choir as I push the candy deeper into her pussy, gripping the curved end of it as I pump it in and out of her.

Using my free hand, I push her thighs wider and position myself between her legs, lowering my mouth to her mound. Swirling my tongue around her swollen clit, the sweet peppermint flavor of the candy coats my tongue. I continue fucking her with the thick stick, lapping up the mix of her juices and the sweetness of the candy. She squirms and moans, so I pick up the pace, fucking her faster, each pump into her wetness removing more and more of the candy's red paint.

Her body convulses with her first orgasm as I suck her clit into my mouth, pinching it between my teeth while I fuck her with the candy cane. Pulling down the fluffy white Santa beard from my face, I don't give her time to come down from the high before pulling out the candy and sucking up whatever juices leak from her hungry little cunt.

Gripping her thighs tightly, I hold her down in her daddy's chair while I devour every pepperminty drop of her like she's my favorite mouthwash and I'm an alcoholic trying to get a little hit while hiding the liquor on my breath. She squirms and moans as she rides my face, but I don't give a fuck. This is for me, not her. Knowing I'll have the sweet juice of the preacher's forbidden daughter coating my tongue makes every second worth it.

Tonight, she's a toy wrapped up just for me in her holiday dress, and Santa Rhett is excited to play.

Gripping her hips, I hold her down as my tongue fucks her minty core. The rotating chair twists and turns, making her pelvis grind on my face as soft, pleading whimpers slip from her swollen lips.

"Yes. Like that," she begs.

Nearing her second orgasm, she removes one hand from the arm of the chair and frees one of her tits from her dress. She pinches her peaked nipple between her fingers, twisting it as her other hand grips the back of my head, pulling my head deeper into her.

I watch her unravel from between her legs as she closes in on her second orgasm. Her long blonde hair nicely done up with perfect spiral curls is now chaotic and hanging down the side of her flushed face.

Grabbing my cock, I stroke it to the speed of my tongue as it glides in and out of her tight hole.

She's close.

I run my tongue up and down her folds quickly before my lips clamp over her clit, and I suck on her. That's all it takes to send her body into a spiral of pleasure. She convulses in her daddy's chair as her orgasm unravels her.

Rising to my feet, I quickly lift her and flip her around, bending her over the back of the chair. The wheels on the small chair roll, knocking it against the preacher's desk as Holly giggles while trying to find balance on shaky legs. I bunch her cute little Christmas dress over her perky ass, getting a clear view in the dim office lighting of her tight little holes. Running my hands around the curve of her ass, I take in its glorious sight. I run the thick candy stick through her folds, watching as her body quivers against the contact, and then bring my hand down hard on her ass. She cries out, her shock echoing around the tiny office.

"Are you gonna fuck me now?" she snaps, bringing her raccoon eyes to mine as she glances over her shoulder.

"Why, Holly? Is that what you want?"

"Yes."

Leaning forward, I brush my lips against her ear as I whisper, "Well, Holly. Naughty girls don't get what they want, and you haven't made it to Santa's nice list yet."

I thrust the thick, sticky candy into her pussy hard and deep. She gasps and her nails dig into the back of the chair as the candy fills her completely. I watch as her ass jiggles in response to each thrust, but it only draws my attention to the prize I *really* want.

I run my thumb in circular motions around her puckered little asshole. I know Holly is a slut behind closed doors, but I can't help but wonder if she's ever given up her *sacred* hole. Continuing to fuck her with the cane, I press my thumb against it, causing her to squirm away. Raising my hand, I bring it down on her ass as hard as I can without inflicting too much bruising. A crimson handprint forms on her fakely-tanned flesh.

"Don't be naughty, Holly. I already told you. Tonight, you're going to do whatever Santa wants, and Santa wants you to ride his fucking candy cane while his thumb fucks your pretty little asshole," I snap, thrusting the candy harder into her tight core.

"Jesus. Fuck," she cries out as she finds her way to another orgasm.

That's *three*.

I smirk, sliding the thick candy stick out as I watch her candy-filled cum leak out of her pussy and onto her daddy's chair. It's an odd sense of pleasure knowing he'll be sitting in his slut daughter's juices while he plans his sermons. Knowing that her preacher daddy will be sitting in this tiny office, meeting with troubled people, claiming to speak the word of God while her cum stains the fabric of his chair.

When Holly finally comes down from the high, she frantically grabs for the chair and the desk in search of something to hold onto, but ends up knocking a bunch of Christmas decorations off, including half of the nativity scene he had set up on his desk, but that's not what draws my attention.

The dim office lights glint off something from the corner of my eye: a strand of red and green tinsel. Grabbing it, I quickly wrap it around her neck, not giving her the time to fight me on it. She might think Santa's done playing, but he's only getting started.

Holly grips the back of the tiny chair and props one leg up to rest on the seat while the other stands. With my tinsel wrapped tightly around her pretty little neck, I grab my cock and run it up and down through her sticky wetness before sliding the tip inside her.

Fuck– for a slut, she's tight.

I pause, letting her tightness choke the tip before I force myself to push my shaft in deeper. Her pussy swallows my cock like a pro, taking each barbell into her until my entire length fills her. Slowly, I retreat, backing myself out, before slamming into her again. As if on cue, the music from the choir changes tune, and "Rudolph the Red-Nosed Reindeer" begins blasting from the speakers. This one was always my favorite as a kid, so I can't help but sing along– I mean, what Santa doesn't join in the holiday spirit?

"You know, *Dasher.*"

With the first reindeer's name, I thrust into her hard and quickly pull out, repeating the process with each and every reindeer named.

"And *Dancer,* and *Prancer,* and *Vixen.*"

I pull on the tinsel reins around her neck as I plow into her.

"God...Yes," she screams, her cries ringing out through her daddy's office.

Reaching forward, I take her chin in my hand, forcing her face to mine. "The only god you pray to when you're on my cock is me, Holly. Understood?"

"Yes-yes, I understand," she replies while panting.

"*Comet,* and *Cupid,* and *Donner,* and *Blitzen,*" I sing, continuing to ram into her. "But do you recall..." I pull on the tinsel around her neck, tightening it until her face glows red from lack of oxygen. "The most famous reindeer of all...*RUDOLPH* the red-nosed reindeer..." I sing loudly as I slide myself out of her.

I hold tinsel reins in my hands firmly as I pound into her, riding her like she's my own personal Rudolph–her glowing face lighting the way to my Christmas orgasm. I fuck her fast and hard as I bring my thumb back to her tight little asshole and circle it again. This time, she doesn't squirm away.

No, this time, she takes it like a good little girl.

"Relax, Holly baby, you're going to like it, I know it," I whisper as I continue to fuck her. "Just focus on Santa's cock like a good girl. You have to get a spot on the nice list. You're *so* close."

I spit on my hand, massaging it around her puckered hole before slowly pushing my thumb inside. I continue to fuck her ruthlessly with my cock, working my thumb in deeper until I'm knuckle deep, and sloppy sex sounds echo around the tiny office.

"Oh fuck... Yes... fuck me," she moans.

"Feels good, doesn't it?" I grunt as I thrust into her. "Santa always knows, baby. I know what every good girl wants," I whisper.

The chair shifts on its wheels as she moves to grip the desk, desperate for something sturdy to hold on to, my aggressive thrusts sending her into her *fourth* orgasm. Her pussy clams up, pulsating around me as she hits her peak and comes undone on my cock. I pull my thumb from her ass and grip her hips as I pound into her.

The desk shakes with the movement, causing her daddy's Jesus snow globe to shake and stir up glitter. The choir's loud chanting fills the room as I lock eyes with the tiny Jesus inside the glass globe.

Come all ye faithful.

The way Jesus's eyes fixate on mine as I pound into the preacher's daughter mixed with the chanting of the choir telling me to come as her tight cunt milks my cock sends me over the edge. I bust, filling every inch of Holly's hole. She whimpers and melts down onto the chair.

Her dress is ruined, her hair is disheveled, and her pussy is leaking a candy-coated mix of our cum.

A knock on the door echoes around the small office, causing Holly to jolt from the chair. Frantically, she does her best to fix her hair before pulling her dress back down. Tucking my cock back into my jeans beneath my Santa suit, I laugh as I watch Holly panic. There's no way someone is coming in here and not knowing what is happening. The office is a mess and reeks of sex.

Christmas decorations are littered everywhere; once neatly stacked papers from the preacher's desk are scattered all over the floor. Holly is a mess. She still has the tinsel wrapped around her neck, but she's more worried about her dress being messed up, for fuck's sake. She's so worried her dear daddy might find out that his precious daughter is one of the biggest sluts around, and it's rather amusing.

"Ye-yes?" Holly, chokes out, as she does her best to fix her hair and makeup in a small mirror she pulled out from her purse.

"Holly? Is that you?" A soft voice responds.

"Sister Gail, hi! Yes, it's me. I'll be right out," Holly calls to the woman outside.

I cross my arms over my chest, watching Holly try to make herself presentable. The sheer panic in her eyes almost has me wanting to bend her over the chair all over again.

"What are you doing in there? Why is the door locked? Your father has been looking for you since he noticed you weren't in your usual seat. Is everything okay, dear?" she questions.

"I-I wasn't feeling well, sorry. I'll be right there, I promise," she explains as she unwraps the tinsel from her neck.

She quickly places it back where I found it and straightens the decorations.

A grin forms on my face as she buckles her strappy black heels around her ankles before picking the pieces of scattered paper off the floor and placing them back on the desk. The Jesus snowglobe splashes about like he's watching her put Daddy's office back together.

"Oh. Well, alright. I'll let him know you'll be right out," the woman says. Her tone is questionable, almost as though she knows Holly is full of shit. Once she's satisfied with her clean-up job, she turns to face me and her lips pull into a smile.

"Don't forget your new favorite toy, you naughty girl," I whisper, nodding towards her daddy's chair where the jumbo candy cane lays.

"Naughty girl? I thought if Santa Rhett got his gift, just the way he wanted, I'd be back on the nice list," she pouts.

Grabbing the candy cane, she strides across the small office until she stands in front of me.

"Ah, but Holly... Why would you want to be a nice girl, when it's the naughty girls that have the most fun?"

She smirks at me before shoving the sticky candy cane in her purse. I cringe as I watch it sink into her bag, but I pull my focus back to her face. Biting down on her bottom lip, she eyes me from head to toe, taking me in one last time before she heads for the door.

"Don't follow me right away," she whispers before leaving to find not only her seat but the facade of the preacher's dutiful daughter.

With Holly gone, I pull out my phone to check the tracking on Jose Demarko's car. It shows he's headed back out of town, so whatever call he got must've been something big. I can't waste any more time if I want to catch up to him. Quietly, I head out of the small office and through the halls until I've made it out the back door.

I toss the sex-scented Santa suit in the back of the preacher's truck bed, lighting up a smoke as I make my way to my bike. I inhale deeply, welcoming the tobacco into my lungs before tossing it aside and climbing on. The engine purrs for me as I rev it up, and I pull on my black matte helmet before popping the kickstand and pulling out into the night.

I don't know where Jose Demarko is going, but now that I have him, I won't lose him.

Working the North Pole

CANDY & ETHAN

It may be Christmas Eve, but it feels like any other night of the year.

My family disowned me when the secret slipped that I'd been stripping in downtown Denver at a new gentlemen's club, The North Pole.

Truth is, I've been stripping for years, and the secret didn't come out until my dad's friend snitched. When he told my dad, he left out the part about paying me for a private lap dance in a private VIP room.

Pathetic piece of shit.

I knew I'd be alone tonight, uninvited to *any* of the get-togethers on either side of my family, so I planned ahead and made sure I picked up a shift to work tonight. It's a

Sunday evening, so it's not my usual night, and I'm not familiar with all of the regulars.

I thought I'd spice things up tonight by wearing a sexy Santa outfit. I've got on a skimpy little red corset and booty shorts trimmed with red faux fur, complete with thigh-high black boots.

Anyone would agree that I look good. I *feel* good.

I always take a couple of shots of vodka before going up on stage. It gives me the liquid courage I need to whore myself out on stage. The peppermint taste of the vodka lingers on my tongue as I step on the stage, taking my spotlight.

The music begins to play, and I sway my body in time with the rhythm. Moving around the pole, I feel its metal curves beneath my hands, feeling the power of my body as I spin faster and faster. The cheers of the crowd encourage me to keep going, my movements never ceasing for a beat.

I grind against the pole, eyeing each of the clients in the crowd. This is my way of ensuring *every* client is a *paying* customer. It makes them feel special when really I'm just reaching into their pockets by eye-fucking them.

My gaze pauses in the far corner of the room, and I notice a man watching me intensely. He's seated, but I can tell he's tall.

He's handsome. Mysterious.

And he appears to be studying my every move. I can't help but feel intrigued, and I'm finding myself drawn to him, instinctually making my movements more seductive.

Alive with energy, my body is empowering me. This is my stage, and I'm determined to show this mysterious stranger my best. It's Christmas Eve after all, and I'm feeling fiery, like I need to show my family what a slut I can be.

Increasing my speed, I spin around the pole, and my long brown hair flies wildly behind me. The crowd whoops and claps in appreciation, but I'm only performing for one person.

For *him.*

My skin tingles as I lock eyes with the strange man, and the air between us sparks with electricity.

The music reaches its climax, and my dancing slows. My body glistens with sweat as I look out over the crowd, flashing a sweet smile at the paying customers. In the corner of my eye, I can see him watching me, and my stomach flutters.

The group of men below the stage begin to disperse, seeking more drinks from the bar between dancers, leaving me alone on the stage to lock eyes with the stranger. For a few moments, neither of us moves. One of my coworkers, Meg, passes by him, and he catches her attention. For a second I feel jealous, until I realize it's me he's wanting. Meg glances up at me, confirming it's me he's talking about. She winks at me, letting me know he's got cash.

The man stands to follow Meg to the back of the club, and she holds up a "four" with her fingers, indicating I need to meet him in room four. She leads him to the bar, then disappears around the corner.

I casually step off the stage, but I'm internally losing my mind over this stranger. The dance I performed for him turned me on more than I'd like to admit. I'm usually pretty numb on stage. It's how I protect myself from some of the disgusting men that come through the club doors, but this man... this man was different.

I make my way to the back, wiggling my way through the growing number of clientele. Room four is the very last room. It's the most *private.*

Entering the room, I'm expecting to find him, but he isn't there yet. The space is small and dark, but the atmosphere is anything but. There's a faint smell of sex in the air, a musky scent that immediately arouses me. I inhale deeply, doing my best to calm my excitement. If this man doesn't want to fuck me... I don't know what I'll do.

Probably take another peppermint vodka shot, then cry on stage. I'm so fucking horny, and it's been a long time since anyone has had this effect on me. We haven't even spoken, yet I need him inside me.

Rough fingertips graze my shoulder, and I jump away from the touch. Turning to find the mysterious stranger, I place my hand over my heart as I say, "You scared me. I didn't hear you come in."

There's a wicked tilt to his lips, and I nearly melt in place. He's even more handsome up close, and his eyes are dark. He's watching me with such an intensity that I don't dare look away.

"I was ensuring our *complete* privacy," he says, his voice low and husky.

My lips curve up, then I suck my lower lip between my teeth, biting down as I watch him. If he was ensuring our "complete" privacy... that means he bought every VIP room in the club. Each room is a thousand dollars, and room four? Room four is three thousand.

This man is *rich,* rich.

"Candy," I quietly introduce myself to him.

"Ethan," he smiles. "I'm here for a good time. Would you like to join me?"

"Well, you paid for me, didn't you?" I ask as though it isn't obvious.

He chuckles low and deep, amused with my attitude. "I did," he nods. "I am asking if you're going to let me fuck your tight little pussy after the way you danced for me."

I can't hide the shock on my face as my jaw drops. I've never had someone be this forward with me, but I can't lie; it turns me on even more.

"Yes," I say confidently.

I've never been more sure of something in my entire life. There's nothing I'd like more than to let Ethan fuck me into oblivion while I wear this skanky little Santa outfit.

His eyes darken at my response, and he takes my hands in his, pulling me closer to him. I can feel the heat radiating off of his body, and my skin lights on fire where our bare skin touches. He's wearing a black button-up shirt and black slacks, held together with a fancy leather belt.

Without a word, Ethan leans in, kissing me with the same hunger I'm feeling, and I welcome him eagerly. His lips are warm, and I allow mine to part for him as his tongue presses against them. The hardness in his slacks is pressing into my stomach, and my hand raises on instinct. I rub my hand over the bulge in his pants firmly, watching his reaction to my touch.

We kiss for several minutes before parting, leaving us both breathless. Running my hands down Ethan's body, I explore every rock-hard inch of him with my fingertips. He shivers as I undo his belt, and then unzip his pants. His cock springs free, and I take him into my mouth.

Running my tongue along his shaft, I lick from base to tip slowly. When I reach the tip, I suck him into my mouth, swirling my tongue over his pink head. His body jerks in reaction, and I smile up at him with my eyes. I pick up the pace, bobbing on his dick and swallowing him down. He's so large that he completely fills my mouth, and I'm salivating. Wrapping his hand through my hair, he pulls my head back, tilting it so I'm forced to stare up at him. He takes his dick in his hand, slapping it on my lips.

"Stand up," he orders, and I don't hesitate to do as he says.

Ethan wraps his hands around the back of my thighs, then lifts me onto a table in the corner. His hands rove my body while his lips skim over my neck and breasts. Yanking my top down, he exposes my breasts. Sucking my peaked nipple into his mouth, he rolls his tongue over it, then flicks it. A moan slips through my lips, and my head falls back as the wetness between my thighs spreads.

Lowering his hands to my shorts, he strips them off of me, leaving me bare and exposed for him on the table.

“So fucking wet,” he growls as he stares at my glistening pussy.

Ethan drops to his knees and then buries his face between my thighs. His hands keep my legs spread wide for him as he devours me, lapping at my clit and running his flattened tongue between my folds. He hums against my clit to the booming beat of the music, drawing out my pleasure.

“Oh, fuck,” I cry out, gripping his dark hair between my fingertips and pulling his head into me as I seek more pressure.

Ethan eats me out, sloppy and wet for several minutes before withdrawing from my pussy. He immediately lines his cock up to my entrance and presses into me. He enters me an inch at a time, giving me time to stretch to his massive dick. We both watch as I take him in, and we’re both panting heated breaths as we anticipate the feeling of him sinking balls deep into my pussy.

He slams into me, and I cry out as the intense pleasure takes over. He thrusts in and out of me, fucking me with the same intensity as the stare he’s been giving me all evening. I match his thrusts as I buck my hips off the table, and the sound of our collision fills the air. Anyone walking by wouldn’t question what we’re doing in here, but he bought out the whole place, and we can be as loud as we want.

"You're such a dirty little slut, swallowing my cock whole with no problem," his harsh words wash over me, and he's speaking my love language.

Degradation.

I *love* when men talk nasty to me, and even more so when they talk down on me when they're fucking me. Perhaps that's why I love being a stripper so much. People look down on me for doing what I do, and they assume I'm the world's biggest slut because of my choice of occupation, but the truth is, this is the first time I've had sex in nearly a year. I spread my legs on the stage, but rarely do I have any real sexual contact with men.

I'm picky, and I'm not attracted to most men.

But Ethan is different. He's hot as fuck and his gaze alone makes me melt. I'd fall to my knees for this man any day of the week.

I explode around him, and stars form in my vision as I ride out my orgasm. He rubs his thick fingers over my clit as I come, drawing it out even longer.

"Fuck!" I scream, clawing at his wrist as I unravel.

As soon as my orgasm subsides, he withdraws from my pussy, leaving me feeling empty without him.

"On your knees," he barks.

Sliding off the table, I fall to the floor, looking up at him as I wait for his cock. He doesn't hesitate to plunge his cock into the back of my throat. His hand forces my head forward, holding me there as he skull fucks me. I can't breathe and there are tears falling from my eyes. I'm gagging, but it doesn't matter. He keeps going and I'm doing everything I can to contain the contents of my stomach.

"Vomit on my cock and I'll fuck your ass without any lube," he threatens, quickening his pace as his grunts grow louder.

He's getting close.

I hold on until I can't, and he removes his dick from my mouth, jacking himself off over my face. I hold my tongue out nice and flat for him, ready to swallow every drop of his cum.

"That's a good little slut," he growls just before releasing himself all over my face.

His cum sprays my face, and I hold perfectly still for him as he finishes, catching every last drop over my tongue.

"Swallow," Ethan smirks as he tucks himself back into his pants.

I do as I'm told, and I drink down every drop of him I can, and I even swipe my finger across a bead of cum dripping down my face. Bringing my finger to my mouth, I close my lips around it, sucking as I swallow.

"Merry Christmas," he grins as he pulls me to my feet, claiming my mouth with his as though he's ramping up for round two.

I could worship this man's cock all night long.

"Merry Christmas," I respond as I run my hand over his already hardening cock. "Merry fucking Christmas."

Sugarplum Party

JADE & JEREMY

A cool chill runs along my back; the breeze from an open window drifts through the bathroom I've sought refuge in. Like an idiot, I cut my finger on a piece of broken glass when I was cleaning up the aftermath of a drunk fae woman.

I'm at the Sugarplum Party, which consists of all types of creatures. Fae, vampires, wolf shifters, and several other species are all here, intoxicated and roaming the halls of the vampire lord's home. I've been hired as part of the clean-up crew. To stay ahead of the mess, I've been making my rounds, tidying the home all evening and picking up stray cups filled with various alcoholic liquids before they're spilled on one of the luxurious rugs.

The vampire lord's home is a grand estate, full of opulent decorations and twinkling lights scattered throughout the ceiling. Vases of his travels line the walls, and every little thing seems to be more expensive than my car.

Several of my friends are here, eager to enjoy a night of drinking and dancing. I would have joined them, but I needed the money to pay the mortgage this month. After both of my parents died unexpectedly in a crash two years ago, I was left to take over their home, and it's been hard.

I'm a single woman making near minimum wage as a phlebotomist in the magical medical center. Overtime is hard to come by when half of the magical community has the ability to heal themselves. I'm one of the few humans living here, but I'm doing my best to fit in.

My finger stings as I run it under icy water, trying to clot the wound and wash away the scent of my blood. Only I would be unfortunate enough to cut themselves open in a house full of vampires. I ran toward the back of the house, where there shouldn't be any guests.

There's a shuffle outside the bathroom door, and my heart begins to pound against my chest as I feel the presence through the door. There's someone there, inhaling my scent through the crack of the door. A cold chill ices over my veins, freezing me in place.

The door knob rattles just as the door opens. I turn around and come face-to-face with Jeremy, the vampire lord. His eyes are dark and molten, and they seem to glow crimson against the twinkling lights in the ceiling reflecting off his tall figure. His skin is golden brown and his lips are set in a grim line.

I can't will myself to move as the lord steps closer. His eyes are locked on mine, and I can feel the heat of his body as he nears me. He smells of a leather and spice mix, and... something else.

Something that makes my heart jump out of my chest.

Jeremy leans forward, focusing his gaze on my cut finger, forcing a shiver of fear to run down my spine.

A soft gasp escapes me as he reaches out, running his fingers along my hand. Grasping my trembling hands, he pulls them to his nose, inhaling deeply.

"I could smell your blood on the other side of the house," he says in a low, raspy voice.

"I'm sorry, my lord. I-I was looking for somewhere private to take care of this before causing a scene."

My pulse races as his eyes seem to darken even more. He's mesmerized by the metallic scent of my blood, and my skin prickles into goosebumps as he inhales again, deeper this time. His eyes flutter, and there's a small smile lighting his face as he takes me in.

Without warning, he grabs my wrist, pulling me out of the bathroom.

"Where are you taking me?" I ask, wide-eyed and breathing quickly.

"To the guest house," he growls, leading me deeper through the house, then out a set of double doors.

We emerge outside, and the stars are shining bright as he drags me across the lawn. We pass the pool, then a small house comes into view. It's larger than the home I live in, and nicer by a long shot. My place looks like a shack compared to this.

"Why are you taking me here?" I cry out, trying to pull away from him, but he's too strong and won't let go. "What are you doing?"

He keeps walking, pulling me along with him until we reach the guest house. He forces the door open, then pushes me inside, locking the door behind him.

Trembling, I look around the room. It's small and sparsely finished. There's a bed in the far corner, and a few pieces of expensive furniture scattered about, but the most striking feature is the large window that opens to the night sky, putting the stars on full display.

The vampire lord walks toward the window and stands there, staring out into the darkness. He seems lost in thought and doesn't seem to notice as I begin to slowly back away from him.

My hand feels warm, and I look down just in time to watch a drop of blood drip from the tip of my finger, falling to the floor in slow motion.

Jeremy's head snaps, turning to face me. His eyes are feral as he smells the blood dripping from my finger. I watch in horror as his body begins to shake.

He steps toward me, and in a low voice he says, "Come with me."

Without another word, he grabs my hand, once again dragging me against my will. He pulls me through the darkness, not stopping until we're far from the party.

This is it. I swallow hard, imagining the whole way that he's going to kill me. Will he even bother to dump my body? Or will I rot in the woods for the wolf shifters to feed on when they're out for a pack run?

We stop in front of an old abandoned building. It looks much more comparable to my home than the last place. I chuckle to myself even though it's the most inappropriate time to be laughing, but I can't help myself. If I'm going to die, I'd rather die semi-happy.

Another cold shiver runs down my spine, similar to the way it did in the bathroom when I washed my bloody finger. This time, it feels... different.

It feels like more than just a cool breeze.

Jeremy opens the door, gesturing for me to walk inside.

At least he didn't shove me this time.

It's a little cabin, musky and damp, and the walls are covered in cobwebs.

Motioning for me to sit down at a small table in the corner of the room, he pulls out a chair for me. He eyes the chair, silently telling me to sit down, and I comply. The chair creaks as he sits across from me, staring at me for several moments before leaning closer.

"I can smell your fear, but I can also smell something else," he pauses, eyeing my hand. "Your blood. It's sweet and inviting. I'm having a hard time resisting the urge to feed off you."

"So you brought me to a cabin in the middle of the wood?" I ask, biting out my words more sharply than I intend. "You thought *this* would solve your lack of self-control?"

Speaking like this to the vampire lord is unheard of, and I bite back the urge to continue. My heart races as I stare back at him. I'm terrified, but I can also feel a strange, forbidden attraction to him.

His long fingers tap against the wood grain of the table, and he's contemplating his response.

Instead of speaking, he leans over the table, then presses a soft kiss to my lips. His lips are warm and hard against mine, making my body shake as a thrilling wave washes down my spine. I catch myself beginning to kiss him back as he deepens his kiss, but I force myself to pull away.

My voice is cold. "What are you doing?"

Time stands still as he glares into my eyes. His red irises are hypnotic, and I'm reminded he has the ability to compel me to do anything he'd like, and I think that's what he might be doing.

I blink, repeating myself when he doesn't answer. "What are you doing?"

He breaks his stare, seemingly defeated. "I want you," he breathes. "Your blood is calling to me, and I must have it."

My breath hitches in the back of my throat.

I can't deny the desire I'm feeling for him, but I'm also scared. The vampire lord is drop-dead gorgeous and alpha as fuck. All the girls drool over him, and here I am, alone with him in the middle of the forest.

Would it be so wrong to let him feed off me? As long as he agrees he won't kill me?

Who am I kidding? He could kill me in a heartbeat if he wanted to... but the vampire lord isn't known for being unnecessarily cruel.

Perhaps he'd let me go...

I've never felt anything like this, and I can't comprehend the mixture of emotions I'm feeling.

Jeremy seems to sense my confusion, and he grabs my hand. "Just for tonight. One feed, then you can sleep in the guest house while your blood supply replenishes, and in the morning you'll be as good as new."

I *should* say no. I *should* stand and leave. I *should* run back to the safety of the house, get in my beat up little car, and get the fuck out of here.

"What do I get out of it?" I ask, eyeing him just as much as he's eyeing me.

A sly smirk spreads across his face. "The orgasm of your lifetime. A night in bed with the vampire lord."

Rolling my eyes, I scoff. "That's a little cocky, don't you think?"

He stands, bracing his weight against the table as he leans over me. His voice lowers as his spice-filled scent hits my nose. "I wouldn't call it little, *princess*."

My jaw drops as my eyes lower to where he's running his hand over the *massive* bulge in his pants. I cross my legs, trying to relieve the pressure building between them.

"Don't hide from me, princess," he repeats his pet name for me. "Not here. We're all alone."

"I'm not... I'm not hiding," I sigh, sitting back in the chair, thinking through the logistics of this arrangement. "How will I get back to the guest house? I won't be able to walk once you feed on me, and we're in the middle of nowhere."

He doesn't hesitate. "I'll carry you back. I'm more of a gentleman than you think," he grins.

His face is devastatingly handsome, and his tanned skin and dark brown hair pull me in. The way he's towering over me makes me instantly wet.

"I can smell your arousal. All you have to say is *yes,* and I'll give you the best night of your life."

"Yes," I blurt before I fully think it through.

I've been telling myself I need to let loose and live a little, and well, this is it. This is my wild and crazy side, and the vampire lord is the first to experience it.

He looks a little shocked, but he swoops me out of the chair in one swift swipe, drawing my body to his. I wrap my legs around his waist, and I can immediately feel his hard cock pressing into me.

There's an old bed beside the table, and he carries me to it, gently laying me on top of the dusty comforter. The bed groans and creaks as our weight sinks into it, and I'm almost worried it's going to break. This isn't the ideal place to spend a kinky night with the vampire lord, but it'll do.

"You're sure?" he asks, raising an eyebrow as he begins working me out of both my pants and panties.

"Yes," I nod, swallowing hard. "One feed, one night."

"You've got it, princess," he smirks as he frees my legs from the confines of my pants.

He moves over me, unbuttoning my white blouse with ease, then helps me out of it. My bra comes off just as easy, and he unclips it with one hand. Tossing my clothes to the table, he begins removing his own clothes. First his dark grey trousers and briefs, then his black tunic.

His body looks as though it's been sculpted by the gods, causing my mouth to water as I watch him. There's a feral hunger in his eyes, and it scares me, but I'm trying to let go.

I'm trying to trust the vampire lord's judgment to know when he needs to stop feeding.

Jeremy drops to his knees beside the bed, then wraps his arms around my legs, pulling my pussy to the edge of the bed, giving himself full access and an unobstructed view. Trailing kisses up my inner thigh, he bites and licks at my flesh. He blows cool breaths against the wet parts of me, making my body shiver.

Flattening his tongue, he runs it through my center, working up and down until he circles my clit, using firm pressure against me as he moves. His tongue is hot in contrast to the cool breath he's releasing on my skin. Moans leave my throat, and my back arches as he devours my pussy.

His mouth leaves my clit, then he sucks on my inner thigh. I can feel the sharp prick of his fangs against my flesh, and a rush of adrenaline begins coursing through me. Reaching for the back of his head, I press him into me, encouraging him to take a bite.

His dark eyes flicker to mine, seeking final consent, and I nod.

My voice is barely a whisper as I shake. "Do it."

Clamping down, his teeth sink into my inner thigh. The pain is sharp, but it's brief and quickly replaced with an overwhelming pleasure. I've heard stories of vampire feedings being insanely euphoric and intense, but this is so much more than I could have ever imagined.

It's deeper than that.

He drinks from me, gulping down large mouthfuls of my blood. The more he takes, the more pleasure I feel. He's moaning and breathing heavily against my body, and I can tell he's enjoying this just as much as I am.

An orgasm builds from the feeding alone, and I cry out as it slams into me, taking me out and unraveling me before I can even realize it's happening.

"Fuck!" I scream, bucking my hips in the air as I come.

Jeremy begins coming back to reality as he slows his feeding, drawing it out in long, shallow mouthfuls. The pleasure changes, and he's building me back up, one gulp at a time.

Bringing his fingers to my pussy while his teeth remain sunk into my thigh, he plays with my folds, spreading my arousal around his fingers before plunging one of them inside of me.

He hooks his finger upward, drawing it out slowly, then pumping it back inside of me. He fucks my pussy with one finger for several strokes, then suddenly inserts a second.

"You're so fucking sweet," he groans against me between swallows. "I don't think one night will be enough."

I couldn't agree more. I'd kill to experience this every night.

That's when I realize his hand is wrapped around his cock, and he's stroking himself while he pleasures me.

His fangs retract, and he rises to his feet, towering over me as he climbs into the bed, scooting me farther up the bed. The hard tip of his cock pokes at my entrance, and I whimper as I wait for him to bury himself inside of me.

A flash of his red irises is all I see before his lips crash into mine. The metallic taste of my blood coats my tongue, and it sends me further into ecstasy.

I feel his hand line his cock up, and he sinks into me just as sharply as his fangs did. His cock is so large it takes me a few seconds to adjust to his girth, but the faint pain soon turns to pleasure as he begins to move, stretching me.

He pounds into me so hard I'm screaming and clawing at his back. I can't breathe as I explode around him. He's fucking me into oblivion.

As I come, he hikes one of my legs over his shoulder, and he fucks me even deeper than before, the curve of his penis hitting me just right with each stroke. Lowering one hand to my clit, he rubs his fingers in firm circular motions to draw out my orgasm, and I'm beginning to black out.

"I can't take it," I cry out, pleading for him to finish before I die.

"You can take it, and you *will,* princess. Now, be a good girl and take this cock."

His hips slow, drawing out each stroke as slowly as he can while keeping his hand on my clit. Tears stream down my face as I come undone once more, immediately after my second orgasm finishes.

The third orgasm tears through me, breaking my soul in two as he picks up the pace, pounding into me with his massive cock.

My pussy clamps down around him, tightening as he fucks me. This sends *him* into oblivion, and he groans loudly as he empties himself into me, nearly collapsing on top of me as he finishes.

"I'll find a rag," he says as he pulls out of me, leaving a trail of his seed dripping onto the bed. "Then we're going for round two."

My head falls back onto the bed, and I sigh contently.

If this is what letting loose feels like, I'll never stop.

Gingerbread Daddy

CASS & ZANE

The late-night breeze bites my face as I make my way up the street, speed walking toward my favorite place, Zane's Bakery. The street is lit by a bright white blanket of freshly dropped snowflakes. I shiver and pull my coat tighter around myself, quickening my pace as I approach the bakery. It's only a few minutes to eight o'clock, and I already know I'm pushing my luck for gingerbread men this late in the evening, but my sister will be here tomorrow morning with my nephew, Jax, and I promised him we'd decorate cookies together.

I've been trying my luck at baking all day, and I ended up losing track of time as I simultaneously lost the battle with homemade Christmas cookies. I can't disappoint Jax after he spent all week talking it up on our video calls.

As I round the corner, approaching the bakery, I'm surprised to find the lights still on. Peering in through the frosty window I can see a tall male figure in the kitchen. Brown skin and deep black curls; my heart flutters at the sight.

Zane, the owner of the bakery.

He's also my secret obsession.

Stepping through the door, the smell of freshly baked gingerbread swirls around my face, and my eyes flutter closed as I inhale the sweet scent. A soft bell chimes above the door as I step through, and Zane turns at the sound.

His warm smile makes me nearly melt in place, but I return the gesture with a grin of my own.

"I was wondering if I'd be seeing you this evening." Zane points toward an oven at the back of the kitchen. "I just put the last batch of gingerbread men in the oven. I don't normally bake this close to closing, but I had a feeling you'd be here."

A few days ago when I was here picking up my weekly order of chocolate chip muffins for the office, I let it slip that I'd be trying my hand at baking for my nephew. Zane knows my history of burnt cookies and fallen cakes, so he spent a few minutes poking fun at me before I had to leave for work.

I didn't think he'd anticipate my failure so accurately, so I'm surprised to hear he had a "feeling" about me.

"Just in time, then," I grin as my cheeks begin to thaw in the heat of the bakery. "I'm looking forward to trying them."

"You'll have to wait a few minutes," he sighs, but I see the less-than-disappointed twinkle in his eyes. "I'm about to close up for the night and lock the doors, but you're welcome to hang out while the gingerbread men bake. It should only be twenty minutes or so."

Alone with the man I spend every second of my free *and* unfree time thinking about? My voice is almost too obvious as I respond, "That'd be lovely."

"Come on in," he waves, gesturing for me to get closer. "Let me take your coat."

Rounding the counter, he's almost jogging toward me. His dark eyes glow against the warmth of a small fire burning in the far corner of the bakery. Before I can respond, his hands are on me and he's helping me out of my thick winter coat. The way his hands innocently glide over my body has me shivering as the fabric pulls away from my body. He steps away to rest it over the back of a chair, and I can't keep my eyes from roaming the toned muscle in his arms.

The air feels heavy.

Thick.

Charged.

Standing side by side in the kitchen, we quietly watch the gingerbread men as they begin to brown. I close my eyes, savoring this moment between us. We've never been more than friends, but I've always wished we were.

I've never made a move, though, and I don't know that I will. I'm too reserved to feel confident enough to put myself out there, and he hasn't exactly shown me enough interest to boost my ego.

Zane glances toward me, and I can't help but smile at him. It feels natural, almost like it's instinctual for my soul to glow in his presence. Comfort settles within me as we stand here, alone in the quiet of the night.

I watch as he opens the oven door and gently removes the fresh batch of gingerbread men. He places them on a cooling rack, and when he turns back to face me, his eyes are shining in the soft light of the oven.

"They're done," he says, his voice low and gentle.

I smile at him, gently touching his arm. "Thank you. I owe you for this. Jax would have been so disappointed if you hadn't stayed late for me."

Zane reaches out and takes my hand in his, his large fingers interlacing with mine. His gaze holds mine; my heart flutters in my chest. Overwhelmingly and suddenly, the bakery seems to disappear around us, and all I can do is stare into his eyes, which look more and more hungry by the second. He looks...

Longing, and lonely.

Without thinking, I lean forward, allowing my lips to brush against his. Zane's arms rise around me, and he draws me close, his lips warm against mine as he presses into me.

Is this real life?

How lucky am I to be on the receiving end of a perfect evening in a bakery with the hottest guy in town, the two of us wrapped in each other's arms as snow glistens outside and the aroma of freshly baked gingerbread men fills the air?

I can feel myself falling further and further into the moment, into the *obsession* I have with this gorgeous man.

Zane deepens our kiss, and I step back against the counter, pulling him with me. Our bodies are pressed together, intertwining as our hands explore the skin hidden beneath our clothing. Zane pulls away, eyeing my body with something I haven't seen from him before.

A tingle runs through my body as his hands roam my body. His gaze is intense: a mix of hunger and undeniable need.

Our kiss deepens and he leans more of his weight into me. Losing my balance, I reach for the counter behind me, attempting to brace myself before I fall. In the midst of blindly searching for something to hold onto, I knock over a measuring cup filled with flour, and it falls to the floor, leaving a cloud of white drifting through the air. The explosion of flour coats us in white powder nearly from head to toe.

"Oh no!" I cry out as it hits the floor, and I'm already looking for a rag to clean the mess I've made. Of course, I would ruin this moment with my clumsiness, it's something I've never been able to get away from. I'm awkward and it leads to too many spills and falls accompanied by the worst timing.

"It's alright, just leave it," Zane whispers against my neck, pulling me back against his rock-hard body.

"Ar-are you sure?" I ask, still eying the space around us for a towel or rag, or *anything* I can use to clean up the disastrous mess I've just made.

He smiles the warmest, most comforting smile. "We can clean up when I'm done with you."

Goosebumps form on my arms. Tonight feels surreal in all the best ways.

"After you're done with me?" I ask, repeating his words back to him.

Exhaling slowly and deeply, he nods. "Yes. I've watched you every day you've come into my bakery, imagining all the things I'd do to you if given the opportunity."

"Why didn't you say anything?" I furrow my brows, frustrated we've both felt this way for such a long time, yet neither of us have ever acted on it. We've wasted so much time keeping silent when we both wanted more.

"You never seemed interested enough and I never felt like it was the right time," he shrugs as he swipes stray hair away from my face, gently tucking it behind my ear. "But this? This feels right. Being alone with you in my bakery on a cold and snowy night feels perfect."

I can hardly contain myself. I feel like I'm going to explode if I don't kiss this man right now.

Slinking my flour-dusted hand around the back of his neck, I pull him into me. There's zero hesitation, zero resistance as our lips collide. His full lips feel soft against mine, and they move with enough rhythm to melt me from the inside out.

Zane grips the back of my thighs, then effortlessly lifts me to a sitting position on the counter. I help him lift my oversized sweater dress over my head before unzipping his jeans. As my fingers slip down his zipper I can already feel the hard length of him pulsing for me, begging to be touched.

His fingertips are hot against my bare flesh, setting my body on fire.

“Is this okay?” he asks, locking his eyes with mine.

“Yes,” I blurt out before I can contain my excitement. “Yes,” I repeat, slightly more calmly to show him I’m being serious and not just irrational in this moment.

I *am* being irrational. We’re about to have sex in his bakery, and there are giant windows lining the storefront which anyone could look through if they were to pass by. How many of his employees have a key to this place? Do they ever stop by after hours?

However, I don’t feel like I’m being irrational in wanting this man inside of me *right now.* I’ve spent endless hours daydreaming of this man and all the things I wanted him to do to me.

He’s now wrong. *This* feels right.

Right here, right now, this is our moment.

His jeans fall to the floor around his ankles, and he kicks them off with his shoes. His black briefs follow shortly after, and his dick springs free.

My eyes widen at the glorious sight. He's hard and ready for me, and there's a drop of precum beading at the tip. I'm not sure how he's going to fit inside me, but I'm determined to make it work.

I didn't wear panties beneath my black tights, and Zane immediately notices. Falling to his knees before me, he spreads my legs wide, devouring the sight with his eyes. A soft moan slips through my lips as he rubs his thick fingers over my pussy.

"Can I?" he asks, tugging at the thin fabric of my tights.

"Yes," I groan as he continues to tease me.

A low growl emanates from the depths of his lungs, then he shreds the fabric, exposing my wet pussy for him. He smiles as the fabric rips away, then pushes my legs apart once more. He dives in mouth first, sliding his tongue over my slick folds, then slowly works his way up to my pulsing clit, circling it in tight, firm motions.

"Ahh," I cry out, letting my head fall back as I grip the thin black curls on his head.

"So fucking wet," he murmurs, pulling back for not more than a second before returning to my pussy.

He's gripping my inner thighs, keeping them parted as I squirm against his face. His tongue darts inside of me, plunging in and out, and he quickly moves up toward my clit where he flicks it over and over again, dragging an intense orgasm dangerously close to the surface.

His hand leaves my thigh, and runs a finger along the center of my pussy, spreading my arousal before slipping it inside of me. I cry out again, racing toward my orgasm.

"I'm going to come," I whimper, thrusting my hips against his hand as I seek more friction.

"Come for me, baby," he moans with his mouth against my clit, sending his vocal vibrations rattling through me.

Picking up the pace, he pushes a second finger inside of me, and I keep meeting his thrusts. I'm fucking his face harder than I probably should be, but it feels so fucking good that I can't stop, and the way he's looking up at me is driving me to keep going.

I unravel, exploding around his fingers as I reach my orgasm. Stars form in my vision, but I imagine they're snowflakes to fully encompass the Christmas spirit.

As I come down from my high, Zane withdraws his fingers, quickly replacing them with his massive cock. He starts with the head, dipping in and out of me an inch at a time as I stretch to fit his wide girth.

"Look at how fucking good you're taking my cock," he praises, never taking his eyes off where my pussy is swallowing him whole.

Zane lifts me from the counter, bracing my ass with his hands to give himself full control of how deeply he enters me. His hips begin to move, pumping into me deeper and deeper with each thrust.

"Oh fuck," I cry out, not caring to mask the volume of my voice.

With my hands tightly wrapped around his neck, I hold my body still in the air as he fucks me. His dick slides in and out, and he ramps up the pace as he gets closer to coming.

Never in a million years would I have guessed how this night was going to end. Zane is balls deep inside my pussy, fucking my brains out in his bakery, and neither of us have a care in the world. In this moment, it's just us.

Cass and Zane.

His grunts get louder as he drives us both closer to the edge. He's slamming me against his body as hard as I can take, and my lust-filled cries get louder as stars begin to cloud my vision. Lifting one hand from my ass, he wraps his fingers through my hair, yanking my head back as he fills me with his cum, using my tight pussy to milk himself dry. My orgasm slows, and I'm panting as I try to catch my breath.

White cum seeps out of me as he slows his thrusts, then withdraws from inside me. Zane gently sets me on my toes, kissing me softly as he reaches for a dish towel. Running it up the inside of my legs, he wipes me clean.

"Same time tomorrow?" Zane asks, laughing as he jokes.

I shrug, smiling as I pull my sweater dress over my head. "I don't see why not."

Zane's eyes narrow in on me, like he's trying to determine whether or not I'm being serious.

And I am.

"I'll be here," he grins, pulling my lips toward him as he grips my chin between his fingers. "Do me a favor, and don't wear panties again. I loved ripping your tights."

"Deal."

Mistletoe Manor

LAURA & LUKE

The night is cold, the air crisp and fresh, cooling my flushed skin and prompting me to draw my thin shawl all the way up to my chin. Snow falls lightly around me, adding to the dreamlike atmosphere in the garden of Mistletoe Manor.

It's mystical, almost *unreal,* as though I've stepped into a world of romance and enchantment, although that's mostly my uncanny ability to over-romanticize nearly everything. The garden is a haven of calm in the midst of a bustling city, and I'm grateful for the reprieve from the hustle and bustle of my everyday life. Being the daughter of a duke can be exhausting.

I was searching for a quiet place to escape to when I stumbled across this spot. The annual Christmas ball is even more overwhelming than usual this year, and I needed to get away. Mother has been forcefully encouraging me to dance with strangers all evening, and I've grown tired of it.

The *one* man who caught my eye early in the night has been surrounded by gorgeous women since the moment he entered the ballroom. I'd never seen him before, but I heard whispers that he's a prince, traveling through the area to strengthen his country's trade agreements.

Doubtful that a prince would want anything to do with me when there are so many proper ladies to choose from, I decided to make an early exit while Mother had her back turned.

I've dreamed of a place like this for so long. Black roses in the midst of winter, soft snowflakes drifting through the air, and a gazebo overlooking a teal pond. The water must be heated because it hasn't frozen over yet.

This spot feels like it was meant for me, like I was meant to find it. The absolute calm it's bringing me is something I've never felt before. There's no mingling with people I do not fancy, there's no Mother to tell me who I can and cannot speak to, and there are no gossipy ladies watching my every move.

I sigh, exhaling slowly as I take in the beautiful sight before me. Snow crunches behind me, and I turn to see the cause of the sound.

A man stands tall with broad shoulders, and his icy blue eyes meet mine as he steps out from the shadows. Dressed in a black coat and matching trousers, his face is partially obscured by the darkness, but I can tell he's handsome with a sharp jawline.

There's something about him that seems almost familiar as if we've met before, and I narrow my eyes on him as he steps closer, trying to get a better view of him.

"Why are you out here all alone, my lady?" he asks. His voice is low and soothing, and yet the faintest trace of an accent hangs in the air.

"I was just... looking for a place to escape to," I admit, shrugging as I adjust my wrap around my shoulders.

He nods as if he understands, folding his hands into his pockets as he takes another step toward me, revealing his face. My jaw drops slightly as I suck in, inhaling a sharp breath.

The prince.

My heart flutters. How did I not notice sooner? The accent should have given it away. It's obvious he's not from here, but it wasn't strong enough to make me think he hasn't spent time in this area.

"My apologies," I say as I drop into a brief curtsy, letting my chin fall forward to avoid his gaze. "Your Highness."

Throwing a hand up, he shakes his head. "No need for formalities, my lady."

"I could say the same," I laugh, speaking before thinking of who I'm talking to.

His eyes sparkle in the moonlight, and I can see a small smirk form on his lips.

I find it peculiar but also relieving that he isn't questioning me further or trying to pry into my personal life. I'm not sure why, but I feel comfortable standing here with him, as if I'm speaking with an old friend.

Turning away from him, I force my attention back to the sparkling lake, watching snowflakes melt away as they reach the surface of the water.

He seems to realize I need some quiet, and he doesn't say anything for several minutes. We stand silently in the gazebo, overlooking the tranquility of the garden. Glancing up at the night sky, I marvel at how the stars twinkle between puffy snow clouds, and how the snowflakes seem to dance around me. It's a sight I'll never forget.

Time seems to stand still as I allow myself to be taken in, consumed by the beauty of the night. I feel at peace, as though all of my worries and troubles are melting away with the snow.

I feel a sudden presence next to me, and I turn to find the prince standing beside me. He's staring at me with a subtle vulnerability in his expression.

"Do you... want to walk with me?" he asks hesitantly.

I think for a moment, then nod my head. "Yes."

He offers his arm to me, and I wrap my hand around it, taking it as we walk together. Our footsteps are muffled by a thin layer of snow as we make our way around the garden. As we walk, the prince tells me his name is Luke, and he's from the country of Altari. He's here to visit an old friend, the owner of Mistletoe Manor.

We speak of many things, but it almost seems as if there's an unspoken understanding between us... As if we are two strangers, destined to meet in this remote garden on this cold and chilly night.

The snow seems to be getting heavier, and it's beginning to stick to the ground more than it already was. We make our way back to the gazebo, seeking refuge from the wet flakes.

Luke looks to the sky, smiling as he says, "Winter is my favorite time of year. There's only one thing I find more beautiful than the crystalized drops drifting from the sky."

My long lashes flutter softly as I watch him. "And what's that?"

His eyes leave the sky to lock with mine. "You."

I laugh lightly, feeling a warmth spread through my chest. I rarely receive compliments and would have never dreamed of such praise from a prince. Not knowing how to respond, I make my way to the center of the gazebo, looking for anything to take my attention away from the warmth rising to my cheeks.

Luke joins me in the center, watching my gaze as it travels. That's when my eyes pause on what I find above us, and he raises his eyes to see it.

Mistletoe.

"It seems rather fitting," he chuckles under his breath.

"Does it?" I smile, returning my gaze to his icy blue eyes.

"It looks as if we were meant to meet here," he says softly.

My heart skips a beat at his words, and for a moment it feels as if the world around us has stopped turning, and we are the only two people in existence.

Reaching up, he touches my face. His hands are warm against my pale skin, and before I know it, his lips are on mine, closing the space between us as he pulls me close.

Our kiss is pure magic, and I feel a fiery passion ignite within my core. The snow is falling around us, heavier by the second, but this kiss is the only thing that matters.

Luke's gentle touch sets me on fire even on this cold winter night.

His pine scent overwhelms me as his body leans into me, lacing itself deep within my nose. I inhale softly, taking in every aspect of this moment. He's so much taller than I am, but we fit together perfectly. His broad frame and large muscles wrap around me effortlessly, making me feel safe.

We kiss for what feels like both an eternity and not long enough, and then he pulls away, eyeing me up and down as though he's savoring the moment, tucking it away in his memory so that he'll never forget it. We're both breathless and panting, but I feel a warmth in my heart, unlike anything I've ever felt before.

I look up into Luke's eyes, and I know, with certainty, that I've found the peace I desperately needed.

Snow Play

CARA & COLLIN

Trudging through deep snow, my coats leave me with next to no protection from the icy chill of winter. The snow hits me mid-calf, and it's a struggle to make it through the thick, white blankets that cover what used to be a path.

Collin and I have been fucking for a few months now, and he surprised me with a romantic getaway in the Colorado mountains. We've been talking about getting away from Iowa for a while, dreaming of finding a moment of peace and quiet in the woods.

We had planned on building a snowman but quickly realized just how deep the snow was. Collin carved out a makeshift igloo for us, and I ran back to the cabin for some blankets. A view of the little igloo forms in my vision, and I reluctantly sigh as I push on, forcing myself to hike through the snow.

"Here," I say, handing out the blankets to Collin as he emerges from the igloo.

"Thanks," he smiles, and he's already eyeing me with the same look he gets when he's horny.

Truth be told, I'm horny too, but I'm not sure about exposing the most sensitive parts of me to the brittle air just to get a quick fuck in.

"Come in," he waves as he quickly disappears into the igloo. "There's no wind in here."

I sigh, reluctantly following him in. I climb through the entrance on my hands and knees, and the wind immediately stops once I'm in the tunnel. My head pops out on the other side of the tunnel where the inside of the igloo opens up, and I come face to face with Collins's erect dick.

"Woah," I gasp as I freeze in place, stunned at how ready he is.

"Suck it, Cara," Collin grins. "Suck it, then I'll fuck that tight little pussy of yours."

I smile up at him from my hands and knees, licking my lips as he bounces the tip of his dick off my lips, spreading around a bead of precum like it's balm.

"Come on, baby," he encourages. "Let's heat up this igloo."

Opening my mouth, I let him slide his dick between my lips, flattening my tongue as it moves toward the back of my throat. I moan as it fills my mouth, using my vocal vibrations to pleasure him. His head falls back as I moan, and his hips buck slightly, forcing his dick to the very back of my throat.

"That's a good girl," he groans through clenched teeth. "Let me fuck your face."

I freeze in place, holding perfectly still as he grabs the back of my head, forcing his dick to the back of my throat, then pulling out just to slam himself into me again. He fucks my mouth fast and hard, and I can't breathe. Tears roll down my cheeks as he thrusts himself inside of me, and I'm on the verge of passing out when he pulls out.

I'm left panting and breathless, gasping for air on my hands and knees.

"Come in," he motions, moving his dick away from my face and allowing me the space I need to crawl all the way inside the igloo.

The blankets I brought are already spread out over the ground, making a cozy little bed for us to fuck on.

How sweet.

I throw myself down on the blankets, wiggling my pants down just far enough to expose my ass and pussy, then I flip over on my stomach, pushing my backside into the air to give him easy access.

I'm already dripping with anticipation as I wait for him to line himself up with my entrance. He slides the tip of his dick through my folds, coating it in my arousal before pressing on my entrance. Pumping himself inside of me an inch at a time, he gives me time to adjust to the fullness. From this position, he hits my cervix with each thrust, and he knows that, so he's excited to get started.

I arch my back as he begins moving behind me, lengthening his stride with each pump. Gripping my hips, he pulls me back against him, using our momentum to bounce off of me, and then plunge back into me in a rhythmic motion.

"Fuck, baby," he hisses. "I love the way your tight little pussy grips my cock."

"Yeah?" I moan. "You love fucking this pussy, don't you?"

He's breathless as he slams into me. "Fuck yeah, I do. Your pussy swallows my cock like it was made for it."

Collin wraps his fingers through my hair, using it as reins to control my body as he fucks me from behind. I lean into his thrusts, meeting him halfway and increasing our speed. I cry out as I get close to coming, and Collin reacts to my pussy tightening around his dick as he plunges inside me deeper, harder, and faster than before.

I'm unraveling, and snowflakes form in my vision as he yanks on my hair, allowing me the opportunity to lose control.

"I'm coming, Collin," I pant. "I'm fucking coming."

"That's right, baby. Come all over this fucking dick for me," he grunts as he strains against me, emptying his load inside me as I come all over him.

Our orgasms mix, slowly dripping down my inner thighs as he pulls out, quickly tucking himself back into his snow pants.

Collin reaches toward my face, gripping my chin between his fingers and forcing my face to his before he says, "You're such a good girl, Cara."

I melt inside. His praise gets me off every single time.

We'll be making *several* trips to this igloo over the weekend.

Whipped by Winters

VANESSA & MR. ANDREW WINTERS

Squeezing my eyes shut, I hold my breath in anticipation as I wait for Mr. Winters to deliver his next strike. My knees quake below me, begging for the relief they so desperately need, but Mr. Winters hasn't permitted me to move yet. I've been bent over this black leather chair for what feels like an eternity, but the reality is, it hasn't been longer than thirty minutes.

Thirty minutes of *painfully* delicious lashings brought on by my employer and dominant, Mr. Andrew Winters.

"Open your fucking eyes," he snaps, the tone of his voice lethal and low as it commands me.

Fearful of what he'll do if I disobey, I pry my eyes open, reluctantly widening one after the other. Dazed and riding a high from the adrenaline coursing through my bloodstream, it takes a moment to adjust to the dimly lit sex dungeon surrounding us.

Crimson lights provide Mr. Winters with just enough light to see what he's doing while keeping most of his whereabouts hidden, leaving them up to my imagination as I quiver and question what his next move will be.

"Yes, sir," I submit, my voice barely a whisper as I watch the dark wall ahead. My nails dig deep into the black leather, puncturing it as I brace myself against the chair, forcing my arms to take the brunt of the weight. My knees are terrifyingly close to giving out, but I refuse to disappoint him.

Not this time.

"If I have to tell you to open your eyes one more time, you'll find yourself gagged and fucked in the ass, Vanessa." He spits my name as though I've betrayed all of his trust.

He approaches me from behind, drawing out each step as he watches me do my best not to unravel before him. I can't see him from this angle, but I know there's a wicked grin spread across that devastatingly handsome face.

The heat between my thighs spreads with each tap of his foot against the cool marble, dripping down my legs as he closes in on my pussy. At this rate, I'll soon find myself straddling a puddle of arousal, and I'm fairly certain he'll make me lap it up with my tongue until his floor sparkles.

"It won't happen again, sir," I apologize as beads of sweat roll down my temples.

When did it get so hot in here?

My heart pounds against my chest, racing at what feels like a thousand beats per second while he takes a wide stance behind me. His peppermint scent fills my nose as he sways his new whip back and forth, practicing all of the precise angles he could spank me. After several forward motions, he settles on how he'll strike me first, prompting a smile only the devil himself could possess.

Chills roll through me as his low voice echoes around me. "Remind me once more, Vanessa. Why must I punish you this evening?"

Trembling in place, I'm hesitant to answer the question we *both* know he knows the answer to, but I proceed anyway. "I was alone in the elevator with Derek."

At the time, I didn't think anything of it as I rode multiple floors with Derek, but Mr. Winters was furious when he saw us step out together shortly after lunch. My punishment began immediately, and he avoided my gaze for the remainder of the workday. Anticipating that he was plotting my punishment, I stayed late until the rest of the office had cleared out. Mr. Winters quickly determined that I would receive one lashing for each floor I passed on the elevator with Derek, a man he has employed for years. Without more than a few short sentences outlining my punishment, Mr. Winters led me to the blacked-out SUV waiting for us at the bottom of the corporate skyscraper. He brought us to his penthouse suite where I was then led to straddle the same position for half an hour.

"Did I give you permission to be alone with another man, Vanessa?"

"N-no," I stutter, shaking my head as I replay the mistake in my mind.

He shifts behind me, scoffing as he strokes the long strands of black leather dangling from the scarlet-handled whip. White faux fur is trimmed around the edges, similar to Santa's red coat. "Then why the fuck did I find you alone in an elevator with Derek?"

I hesitate, trying to determine what might be the best response to the venom leaving his lips.

Before I can form words, he abruptly continues, "Eight." He pauses for a moment, clearly for enhanced dramatic effect. "Eight *fucking* floors you rode with him, and for that, you will receive eight lashings."

He dislikes when I disobediently speak out of turn, especially when he's in his dominant role–and even more so when correcting my bad behavior–but I can't help myself when I'm on the brink of so much pain.

"*You* were in your office alone with Mikayla when I arrived this morning. How is that any different?" My words sound just as spiteful as his. I know I should stop and beg for forgiveness, but I shove all logic to the side and keep the momentum going. "How is *that* not ten times worse than what I did?"

I hear the not-so-amused smile crack on his lips behind me, and before I can brace myself, he strikes his whip against my bare ass, using as much muscle as he can manage without losing control. The small of my back arches in response as I cry out in pain, the sting ripping through my spine.

"Three," he counts aloud. Anger radiates through his throaty tone. "Hold your tongue, or I'll follow through with my threat to fuck your ass."

My mouth clamps shut, and I don't dare say another word. Anal is my *one* hesitation, and I almost listed it as a hard limit when we discussed our arrangement. Still, I couldn't bring myself to take anything off the table at the risk of disappointing Mr. Winters. I most certainly do *not* want to engage in anal play when he's in such a sour mood.

The next lashing cracks against my pale flesh not long after I've straightened myself back out, and it burns just as much as the last.

"Four," he continues once I've regained minimal control of my limbs. "If it isn't already abundantly clear, you will not allow yourself to be alone with any man other than myself without seeking prior permission."

He's being ridiculous, and we both know it.

I can't control who I'm around at work, especially when he employs so many type-A alpha males, and how incredibly unprofessional would it be for me to purposefully avoid men in the workplace? We said we wouldn't let our arrangement interfere with work, but we've let it seep into our daily lives in more ways than one. I've lost count of how many times I've let him call me to his office, lock the door, and fuck me over his desk between conference calls.

But this is taking it too far. This is my *career* we're talking about.

I begin shaking my head in disagreement, ready to argue with him.

The satin swish of his button-up shirt freezes me in place, indicating he's about to deliver his next blow. "Do you understand?" he asks, his words deceptively smoky and sweet like he isn't already holding the whip high above his head.

I silently nod to avoid being struck but hold my tongue out of frustration. It's not until I feel the flick of the leather sliding against the back of my thighs that I realize he's dropped his arm and is preparing to strike me again. "Yes," I say quickly, swallowing hard. "I understand."

"I'm asking you a question, Vanessa," he barks my name patronizingly as though he's my father reprimanding me for disobedience. "Are you sure you're listening?"

I nod again, even more annoyed, but also incredibly terrified of the whip he's holding.

A moment passes. No strike.

"I *asked*," he emphasizes the word to demonstrate how unimpressed he is with my inability to speak, "if you understand."

He's growing impatient, and I'm unintentionally pushing his buttons.

"Y-yes, I understand, sir."

"Good," he says, lowering the whip to rest at his side. "Now, bend over the bed."

Rattled by the rollercoaster of emotion emanating from Mr. Winters, I force myself from the chair and onto the bed a few feet away, leaning forward as I press my torso against the plush comforter.

Silently, he steps around me, his suede shoes padding against the cold floor. His presence alone is enough to suck the air from my lungs, leaving me speechless. He doesn't need to speak for me to *feel* his dominance. He *is* dominance.

I close my eyes, inhaling deeply as I prepare for the next strike.

I expect him to deliver it immediately after arranging my arms by my sides, but he doesn't.

"Vanessa," he breaks the stillness.

I open my eyes at the sound of his voice, turning to find him standing behind me, watching me with his thick whip slung over his shoulder. There's a softness in his eyes I hadn't expected, and I feel like he may be playing games.

"What?" I hiss as I begin to lose patience, rotating my face away from him. "You know what? You're right. I should have gotten permission first." I can't stop the sarcasm as it rolls off my tongue. "I *should* have made an unsuspecting coworker feel uncomfortable because of this secret arrangement we've made outside of work."

Even though I'm facing the bed, I can see him roll his eyes through my peripheral vision, and he's shaking his head.

"I don't give a *fuck* about Derek. I don't give a *fuck* about work, or the company, or even your fucking job," he growls, unfastening his belt as he lets it drop to his feet. "But you will learn your place."

The whip slides from his hand, landing on the bed beside me, a wordless warning to keep my damn mouth shut. His bare hands glide over my bare skin, his fingers running over my tortured and raised backside before finding their way up my body, eventually landing on my breasts.

His pants drop to a pile at his feet as he releases a sharp breath behind me. "This," he continues, squeezing my breasts against his palms. "*This* is what I care about."

He leans around me, forcing my face toward him as he firmly grasps my chin between his thumb and index finger, pressing his mouth to mine to kiss me deeply before pulling back.

"*This*," he purrs, tracing his fingers along my core, "is what I care about."

His hand stops just short of my clit, and I yearn for him to touch me like he's done so many times before.

"*This*," he whispers, his fingers parting my folds to explore my wet center, "is *all* I care about. Don't you know that?"

I bite my lip, holding back my moan as his hand slides over my pussy, spreading my arousal over my clit.

He retracts his hand, smacking against my thigh. It stings, but he knows how to ride the line between pleasure and pain.

Sweet. Blissful. Pain.

"Answer me," he demands.

"Yes," I reply breathlessly. "I know."

"Good girl," he praises. "Lay on your back and spread your legs for me," he says, taking his cock in his hand.

"Yes, sir," I squeal, perhaps a little too excited.

I turn over, spreading my legs as far as they go. He wastes no time as he pushes his cock inside me, gripping my hips and driving himself into me as deep as he can go.

"You are mine," he says again, hungrily thrusting into me. "You are mine, and I own you. Now, say it."

"Yes, sir," I cry out between thrusts, knowing it's exactly what he wants to hear, what he *needs* to hear.

"Tell me," he grunts beneath his breath, using his weight against me as he continues driving into me. "Tell me you're mine. I need to hear you say the words."

"I'm yours," I whimper, quickly closing in on an orgasm. "I'm yours," I repeat unexpectedly. "I'm yours. Only yours."

My words electrify him, washing over him in prideful waves. He picks up the pace, and my body tightens around his cock.

He pushes me further into the mattress, and my legs flail in the air as I grip the sheets below me.

"Come," he commands, sliding an arm beneath my waist, angling me into an even more pleasurable position. "Come with me."

My body shakes as I let go, and my pussy clamps down around his cock.

The increased pressure throws him into an orgasm just as intense as my own, and he unravels, emptying himself inside me. His strokes slow into long, forward motions, and he gives me a soft slap on the ass before pulling out.

Crossing the room, Mr. Winters finds a clean rag in a fully stocked dresser. He quickly cleans himself up, then turns back toward me.

My legs are still spread wide, waiting for him to wipe me down. Mr. Winters makes quick work of tidying me up, then pulls me by the hand, tugging me off the bed.

"Let me wash your body in the shower," he whispers against my ear, holding me closely while planting a trail of soft kisses down my neck.

I've only received *half* of my punishment, but I don't dare mention it. He knows, but he's feeling temporarily satisfied and okay with what he's delivered. Now isn't the time to question him, it's the time to follow his lead and let him worship my body in a steamy shower.

The Naughty Elf

KIRA & DASH

I've worked in Santa's workshop for as long as I can remember, serving the children of the world day after day. My life is devoted to the shop, and for that, I cannot have relationships outside of my immediate family.

No flirting. No dating. No marriage.

And *certainly* no fucking.

Not a day has gone by where I haven't felt a flutter of excitement as I walk through the warm workshop doors. I've never been quite sure why I love it so much—maybe it's the sense of purpose and belonging that it gives me or the knowledge that I'm playing an important role in making the world a better place.

But lately, all of that seems so pale in comparison to the feelings that one person gives me.

Dash, the elf boss.

He's nothing like the other elves in the workshop—he's tall and strong, brave and bold, and has a presence that seems to make everyone around him a little bit nervous. He has a commanding aura that fills the room, and when he speaks, everyone listens.

I'm completely enthralled by him, and I have a hard time keeping my eyes off him when he's in the same room.

He's everything I've ever wanted in a man, and yet, he's my boss, and I've sworn to devote myself only to the workshop, just as every other worker elf has. Relationships of any kind are forbidden, which means I've had to keep my feelings for Dash to myself, no matter how badly I've wanted to be with him.

But... I can't help myself. Every time we're in the same room, my heart pounds a little faster and my stomach flips with anticipation. I know it's wrong to feel this way for a man, especially my boss, but I can't help that I feel this way.

It's only natural to want love, to want another's touch.

This is what I dread most about my job— the moments when I'm reminded of what can't be, but I can't deny my feelings anymore. I'm dreaming of a different life, one where Dash and I are together in a beautiful home with children running around, a future full of hot cocoa, love, and laughter.

It's a dream I know I shouldn't make reality, and yet it's all I have.

Moving silently around the workshop, my little feet shuffle lightly against the wooden floorboards as I hurry to do my tasks. I can feel Dash's eyes upon me, and his gaze is heavier than the air itself. A shiver runs down my spine, and I pause to glance back at him over my shoulder before quickly turning away. He's leaning against the wall, his toned and muscular arms crossed, and watching me with a heated gaze that makes my stomach quiver.

I *know* the attraction between us is forbidden. I *know* I shouldn't feel the way I do about him, yet our connection is undeniable.

"Kira," Dash's voice is heavy, laced with a deep, raspy tone that makes me quiver inside. "It's late. We should go."

I nod, my heart pounding against my chest as I slowly walk to the exit with Dash on my heels. My heart is thumping, and I'm barely able to contain my anticipation as we exit the workshop, stepping into the darkness of night.

There's a chill in the air as we step outside, making my overly sensitive skin pimple with goosebumps. I realize I've forgotten my coat, and I turn too quickly to retrieve it. I bump into Dash, who is directly behind me, dark-eyed and hungry.

"Oh, I'm sorry," I apologize, taking a step back.

Dash matches my step, closing the distance between us. Reaching for my face, his hand gently cups my chin. My eyes close and my skin prickles with desire as his thumb strokes across my cold cheek. Feeling powerless as he pulls me closer, I let him hold me with our lips only inches apart. The warmth of his body against mine feels *so* good, and I'm desperate for more.

"We shouldn't be doing this," I murmur, though my words only seem to encourage him as his lips crash against mine in a hungry need and his hands begin roaming my body.

I don't pull away, and our kiss deepens. My breathing becomes heavy as Dash's hands explore the curves beneath my uniform. His fingers work their way lower, pressing against the fabric of my skirt, and I gasp against his lips.

I've never done this before.

It's forbidden.

He shouldn't have done this before either, yet his lips move as though he has years of experience.

Dash pulls away, and I feel as though I'm going to faint from the intensity of his gaze. "Kira," he growls, his voice a deep whisper. "I can't keep away from you any longer. I *need* you."

His words send a shiver down my spine, and I can't deny the truth. I feel the *same* need, and as he pulls me closer, my body seems to melt into his.

We stumble back into the toy shop, neither of us paying mind to the tools and toys that scatter to the floor in our wake. Dash presses me against a table, his mouth finding mine once again as his hands caress my body. A soft moan slips through my lips as pleasure ripples through me, and Dash responds with an even deeper, more passionate kiss that makes me forget everything but the pleasure that I'm feeling.

I feel his hand work its way beneath my skirt, making my breath hitch in the back of my throat, and I let out a gasp as his fingers brush against the heat between my legs.

"I can't deny myself of your body any longer, Kira," Dash breathes through shallow breaths. "I see the way you watch me. I see the way you *need* me."

"I-I didn't think you'd noticed me," I confess.

"Of course, I noticed you, Kira. I've never stopped watching you since the moment you walked into my workshop. I've craved you for years, and I can't stop myself any longer."

"But our devotion," I remind him. "To the workshop. To Santa."

"Fuck the devotion," he curses, sending chills through me.

I've never heard any of the worker elves curse before, and I certainly never thought it would be Dash to bring such words to my ears. I have to admit, it turns me on even more than I already am, and I feel my clit begin to pulse beneath my skirt.

Dash's hands begin moving again when he sees the look on my face, confirming my feelings for him and my need to forget my devotion. A shuddering cry falls from my mouth as he slips his hand beneath my panties, rubbing his fingers over my wet pussy. My senses are spinning out of control and I can barely breathe.

The pleasure is surreal, and I'm dizzy with the euphoric high I'm feeling.

His body shifts against mine, pressing his hard cock against the side of my leg as he grinds. He's so hard it almost hurts me to have it pressed against me so hard, so I can only imagine how badly it's hurting him to not be relieved with my touch.

Moving his hand to my waist, he presses me down on the table, and his lips find mine once more as he moves against me. His hard muscles shift as he moves, and the sensation makes me gasp.

I want more.

I *need* more.

My hips arch against him as his hands explore my folds, sliding around in my arousal until he finds my clit, then works two fingers in firm, circular motions. It feels almost unbearable, and that's when my body begins to unravel, exploding around his fingers as I cry out in pleasure.

"Dash," I scream, not caring to quiet my voice from wandering ears.

We should be the only two left in the workshop. I stayed late to finish extra work because we're short-staffed and because it gives me an excuse to be alone with Dash in the workshop. I've daydreamed about moments like this for so long, but I never actually thought they'd become a reality.

My hips buck against his hand, seeking even more friction than what he's giving me, fighting through the slight pain of being stretched for the first time.

"Are you going to come for me, Kira?" Dash's voice leaves me breathless. "Do you like the way my hand fucks your tight little pussy? You're such a naughty little elf."

His mouth ravages mine as he dips a finger inside me, moving in a hooking motion as he pumps in and out of me. I can feel myself spiraling towards release, my body quivering and shaking as pleasure sweeps through me.

The clink of metal fills my ears, followed by the sound of Dash's trousers being unzipped. Just as I'm about to come, Dash moves my panties to the side and replaces his fingers with his cock, thrusting inside of me with enough force to knock more toys off the workshop table. They hit the ground, clinking and chiming as they scatter across the floorboards.

Dash plows into me with a hunger I've only dreamed of, and we're quickly losing control. The table continues scooting across the workshop as he thrusts into me. He's grunting and groaning while he fills me, watching my pussy swallow him whole.

My head falls back when I can't take any more, and I come all around him, forcing me to shake as an orgasm rips through me. Dash follows close behind me, his climax intensifying as he moans my name.

Shuddering as the pleasure slowly subsides, I collapse against the table with the weight of Dash's body against me. For a moment, all that existed was the two of us, and I now realize that no matter how forbidden our love may be, I never want to let him go.

Garland Gag

ERICA & STERLING

WRITTEN BY MELISSA MCSHERRY

I was overjoyed when Sterling invited me to spend Christmas with his family. I've been waiting for *months* to not only see the tiny town he once called home but also to meet his mother.

My soon-to-be mother-in-law.

I'm not sure what I expected our holiday trip to be like, but I definitely didn't expect to be making out like a couple of college kids next to the fireplace in his mother's living room.

However, I will admit I've been pleasantly surprised by the sheer beauty of his family home. Its old country charm had me mesmerized the moment I saw it. It's such a refreshing feeling after living in the hustle and bustle of Chicago for so many years.

Laying on top of me, Sterling deepens our kiss as he settles himself between my legs. Beneath the thick, old-fashioned Christmas quilt his grandmother made, I can feel his erection rubbing against my core. My nightshirt hangs off my shoulder, exposing my skin to the heat of the roaring fire next to us.

He trails soft, weak kisses down my jaw and neck, working his way to my collarbone as his hand runs beneath my shirt. Everyone turned in for the night hours ago, and the house is silent, but the crackling of the fire and our heavy breaths seem so much louder to my nervous ears.

"What if she hears us?" I mutter, breaking the kiss briefly.

He smirks with that goddamn handsome mouth of his before returning his lips to mine. "That's half the fun, babe," he whispers.

Easy for him to say.

"I don't want to give your mother any reason to hate me more than she already does, Sterling."

"She doesn't hate you," he laughs, trailing his kisses down my jaw and neck. His hands work their way down my body, and he tugs on my silk night shorts—his way of telling me to take them off.

"You're overthinking it. Did you see how much wine she drank at dinner? She'll be passed out cold till morning. Now take these off."

"Absolutely not," I laugh.

He's wrong. I may have just met her, but I can already tell she isn't my biggest fan, and finding us screwing on her expensive-ass rug definitely wouldn't help my case. As if the decor choices in her home weren't sign enough of how old-fashioned she is, the look she gave me when I showed up in my low-cut Versace dress tonight confirmed it.

Sterling pulls on the thin silk of my night shorts again as his kisses continue down my collarbone until he reaches the swell of my breast. He looks up, turning his darkened eyes to mine as he trails his lips across the fabric that covers my breasts, flicking my peaked nipple with his tongue. Shock waves of pleasure course through my body as I look down on him teasing me. The thought of being caught builds a familiar need between my legs.

"Fuck..." I hiss. "Sterling, we can't do this. Not here!"

He ignores my weak protest, a cocky smirk forming on his lips as he continues lower down my body. He plants soft kisses and flicks his heated tongue along my stomach and hips until he reaches my pelvis, where he pulls on the waistband of my shorts with his teeth. When he lets go, the elastic waist snaps back against my stomach, sending a sharp chill down my spine. His hands grip my hips firmly over my night shorts before he runs his tongue across my silk-covered pussy. My back arches off the blanket-covered rug, and a moan slips from my lips that echoes around the empty main floor of the old house.

I panic. My hand snaps to cover my mouth in an effort to silence myself.

"Sterling, babe," I whisper as I grab him by the chin, forcing his eyes to mine. "Can we at least take it to the bedroom, please?" I beg.

Sitting back on his knees, he locks eyes with mine as he grabs the thick faux cedar garland that hangs across the mantle of the massive stone fireplace and pulls it down, sending small wooden Christmas figures crashing to the floor as it falls.

"Are you crazy? What are you doing?" I question as I watch him, dumbfounded by how little he cares about waking his mother.

He leans forward, brushing the tip of his nose against mine before moving his lips to my ear.

"I want to taste you here. Now. I don't care who might walk in." he whispers before wrapping the garland tightly around my neck and mouth, silencing my protests before running his hand along my body.

I choke and gasp as I walk the thin line between fear and pleasure. I watch quietly as he inches his hand inside the unbuttoned part of my nightshirt. He speaks so casually, almost as though we're back home in our tiny apartment and not at risk of being caught by his mother.

Unable to speak with the garland clenched around my throat and my air intake limited, I can't think. I can only *feel*, which is precisely what Sterling wants. As a pleasure dom, my pleasure is his pleasure. Gently, he runs his thick fingers over my pussy, pulling my silk shorts to the side. My hips instinctively rock into his touch, craving more when I know I shouldn't.

"Good girl," he whispers, his lips curving into a wicked grin.

Pulling my panties to the side with my shorts, he lowers his mouth and runs his hot tongue through my folds. My body shudders, and muffled moans slip from my lips. The adrenaline coursing through my body has my senses heightened, making every touch so much more intense. He laughs cockily, enjoying every minute of the pleasurable torture he's inflicting. With the ends of the garland in his hands, he grips my hips tightly, holding me down while his tongue swirls my sensitive clit in tantalizingly slow, circular motions.

Teasing and working me up all while he's working himself up, too. This is what he likes. To dominate and to pleasure me as much as possible. Sometimes more than I can handle, but that doesn't stop him. Nor do I.

But tonight, as good as his tongue feels, and as badly as I want to ride his handsome face until I find release, I can't bring myself to forget how little privacy we have here on his mother's living room floor.

Sterling nips and sucks at my clit, causing my body to spasm and twitch in his grasp. My hands grip his thick, dark hair as I pull him into me, guiding his mouth to where I need him the most. His hands slide around to my ass, gripping me by my round cheeks as he lifts my hips, bringing me to his mouth.

He devours me.

Right there in the glow of the crackling fire in his mother's living room.

My mother-in-law's living room.

The creaking floorboards above us draw my attention, and I panic. Desperate to escape his clutches for fear of being caught, his grip only tightens on me, holding me right where he wants me. Sterling continues his pleasuring assault. His tongue slides in and out of my tightness as he laps up my arousal.

I constantly turn my eyes on the stairs in the main hallway, terrified his mother will make her way down them in search of a midnight snack or a glass of water, only to find her son's head buried deep between my thighs.

I begin to see stars as my vision dims from lack of air. Pleasure builds, mixing with my fear. It's a new feeling, but one I find myself enjoying more than I expected. Silenced moans slip from my lips as my hands rush to the garland around my neck. I can feel my orgasm coming before it hits me. One of my hands slaps the thick stone base of the fireplace as it rolls over me.

My body quivers, and my legs clench around his head as he buries his tongue inside me, tasting my release. Grinding my hips on his face, I ride out my first orgasm while Sterling licks and sucks up every drop. He places me back down softly on the blankets. My chest rises and falls rapidly, my lungs never able to intake the air they so desperately crave with the garland wrapped around my throat.

"Fuck, Erica. I could cum just from watching you come apart for me," he whispers before bringing two of his thick fingers to my mouth. "Suck on them, babe."

I do.

Opening my mouth, he slides them past my swollen lips, and I close my mouth around them. He watches, a shiver rocking through him as I swirl my tongue around them, coating them in my saliva before allowing him to pull them out.

One thing I've learned in our months together is that although my body feels like it's done, it isn't. No matter how tired I am, or how many orgasms he's milked out of me, Sterling manages to find another one. This is just as much for him as it is for me. Making me cum as many times as he can is *his* version of foreplay.

Sterling runs his spit-coated fingers across my sensitive core, spreading my juices around before he slides one finger inside me. I watch with hooded eyes as he fingers my tight pussy. He starts off slow, stretching me out before sliding in a second finger.

My back arches off the floor, and my eyes roll into the back of my head as he moves his fingers in a hooking motion, hitting the spot he knows I love. Muffled moans fill the room, mingling with his quickened breath.

"That's a good girl. Give me what I want, Erica."

The floor above us creaks again, and my eyes snap open. Frantically, I pull at the garland around my throat.

Does he not hear it, too?

My widened eyes lock with his as a smirk forms on his face. He hears it, but he doesn't care. If anything, it's turning him on more knowing we could be caught at any moment... I admit it intensifies things a bit.

With every pump of his fingers and creak of the floorboards, I'm reminded of just how exposed we are. Of just how easily his mother could walk in and find us like this. There's a certain thrill to it, and although I'm nervous, I'm starting to love it.

Bringing his garland-filled hand to my pelvis, he presses down before picking up the pace with his fingers. Every hook of his fingers hits my G-spot like a pro.

He should be by now. No one has ever known my body as Sterling does, but then again, no one has ever made it their mission to please me the way he does.

Pressure builds between my legs, each pump of his fingers bringing me closer to the edge of my second orgasm. I try to clench my legs closed as the intensity grows, but he doesn't allow it, forcing my thighs back open as a guttural chuckle rumbles through his chest.

"Not happening. You know what I want," he whispers. "Give it to me Erica. Cum on my fingers."

My orgasm hits me like a tsunami. Chills run up and down my spine as my body convulses. Silent moans and gurgled sounds echo around the silent main floor of the house as his fingers slow their pace, pumping in and out of me while I ride it out. Specks of stars fill my vision, mingling with the twinkling lights of the holiday decor around the room. I pull at the garland again, desperate to fill my lungs with much-needed air. Seeing my dilemma, Sterling loosens it. I gasp for air, my chest rising and falling rapidly as my eyes flutter closed.

Before I can fully come down from the high, his hard cock is lined up at my entrance. Shocked, I push myself up on my elbows, where I meet his cocky grin. He runs the tip through my wetness before pushing it in a tiny bit, then pulling it back out, teasing and playing all while knowing every second of it is pure and utter torture for me. Biting down on his bottom lip, Sterling watches as he slides himself inside me, and pulls himself back out. Slow, deep thrusts as he rolls his hips into me.

"Fuck..." he hisses as he slams into me again.

A whimper escapes me, causing him to pull on the garland, tightening it around my throat again. This time I welcome it knowing just how hard it makes me cum to ride that fine line.

"More, Sterling," I choke out against my better judgment.

"Yeah? You want more, babe? You like when I play with you, don't you?" he grunts as he fucks me.

His cock slams into me hard and deep, pushing my back into the blankets that cover the floor. I try to respond, but the garland tightening with each thrust makes it impossible. I nod, turning my pleading eyes to him in the hopes that he'll understand.

"You like knowing we could get caught, don't you? Damn... you feel so fucking good."

With the garland wrapped so tightly around my throat again, my voice is no more than a gargled sound while my third orgasm hits me. I grip the garland tightly at my throat as Sterling pounds into me. Sloppy sex sounds fill the air.

"That's right, baby. *Fuck*. God, I love when your pussy squeezes me like that." he praises with a grunt before he spits, and his warm saliva lands on my pussy, mixing with my cum mid-thrust.

He doesn't relent. Sterling has stamina for days, but when I lock eyes with him, I can tell he's close, too.

Harder.

Every roll of his hips brings him deeper inside me. My hands find his chest and I slide them under the cotton fabric of his t-shirt. His chest is coated in a thin layer of sweat as I claw my fingers down it, feeling every muscle tense and shift as he fucks me. He rams into me one last time before finding his own release and filling me with his warm cum. A deep moan escapes him and his pace slows as he fucks his cum into the deepest parts of me. The feeling of his throbbing cock emptying inside me is almost enough to send me over the edge again. He loosens the garland, removing it from my neck and tossing it to the side before bringing his lips down to mine.

"I told you we wouldn't get caught. You were all worried for nothing," he whispers, brushing the tip of his nose with mine.

I inhale deeply, filling my lungs with the air they spent the last half hour craving as a small giggle escapes me. Lowering himself to the crook of my neck, we lay like that for a few moments, both coming down from our highs. Looking around the room, I find that the once-roaring fire is no more than a few glowing embers.

Slowly, Sterling slides out of me and lifts himself to kneel above me. I watch as he lifts his shirt over his head before bringing it between my legs.

"Babe, no," I protest, doing my best to remain quiet.

"Relax. It's better my shirt than my mother's blankets, don't you think?" he laughs.

He's right. It's bad enough I will have to spend all of tomorrow trying to keep a straight face while they sit beneath the blankets I just got fucked on. I watch as Sterling wipes his shirt across my overly sensitive flesh, causing me to twitch and jump before he fixes my panties and shorts.

"All clean," he whispers, bringing his lips to mine. A smile forms on my lips knowing he tended to me before even tucking his cock back into his pants. "Now, let me get us some hot cocoa."

"That would be perfect," I smile.

"Shit, let me get a new log for the fire first, I didn't realize it had burnt down already."

"Well, I mean, you were rather busy," I add with a smirk.

"And I enjoyed every second of it."

I watch as Sterling stands and grabs a thick log of cedar from the pile next to the stone mantle. Grabbing the poker, he stirs up the embers, causing them to glow a bright red before placing the log on top of them. It doesn't take long for the embers to catch onto the dry wood, and for the once-dead flames to return, roaring to life and casting their heated glow over me.

While he finishes with the fire, I begin picking up the small decor that was knocked down with the garland, placing it all back where I *think* it belongs. I drape the thick garland across the mantle, knowing tomorrow when

I see it I'll be thinking about how it felt wrapped around my neck and mouth, gagging me while he fucked me right here on the living room floor.

Wrapping the throw blanket around me, I smile at Sterling before he heads off to the kitchen to grab us hot cocoa. My eyes fixate on the flames as my thoughts trail back to everything that's happened tonight. It's crazy to think how I spent so many months being so nervous to meet his mother, only to end up being fucked on her floor while she slept above us. I find myself hoping that the floorboards I heard creaking were just the sounds of an old house shifting, and not her. Tomorrow will be crazy enough, never mind having to face his mother if we woke her up with our crazy night of sex.

My pussy still throbs from this round. I never thought the fear of being caught could intensify things so much. That, with the added mix of air loss from his mother's garland. Sterling enters the living room behind me, carrying two steaming marshmallow-topped mugs of hot cocoa. Reaching me, he carefully hands me mine before lowering himself to sit next to me.

"What were you thinking?" he asks.

I blow on the steaming drink as a smile forms on my lips. "About how interesting tomorrow is going to be."

"Oh, it will be fun. House full of distant family, drinking, kids running around. You know, now that I know you get off on the fear of being caught, maybe tomorrow I can bend you over the sink in the powder room." he adds.

Shocked, I turn my widened eyes on him as my jaw drops. "Absolutely not!" I whisper, elbowing him in the ribs.

"Why not? I mean, at least it would be an easier cleanup," he chuckles.

"You're horrible!" I laugh, bringing the mug to my lips.

I swallow down the sweet chocolatey liquid, welcoming the warm feeling it fills me with. We spend a few minutes talking as he tells me about his childhood and growing up here. I find myself in awe with how different things are here compared to back home, but by the sounds of it, it's a beautiful place to raise a family. It's hard for me to picture him living in a place like this when I see how naturally he fits into the corporate world and big-city life.

Once Sterling is done, he takes our mugs, placing them on the thick stone base of the fireplace before wrapping an arm around me and pulling me into him. All thoughts of tomorrow dissipate as he holds me close, and we fall asleep in the fire's glow.

On Donner, On Vixen

AUDREY, LANCE DONNER, & ADAM VIXEN

My heels click against the office floor as I walk down the halls of the office, Lance Donner and Adam Vixen in tow. Their expensive suede shoes echo behind me as we close in on my office. The air hangs heavy around us, and I'm feeling confident with its weight.

I've been looking forward to the Christmas party all week, but now the thrill of mingling with high-level executives has been replaced with the excitement of something entirely different. I have an agenda, and I'm ready to put it in motion.

The three of us keep our heads low and eyes peeled for nosy workers as we walk in silence. We slipped away from the party unnoticed, leaving one at a time, and then grouped up just down the hall. None of us wanted to draw attention our way, arousing suspicion about our sudden departure from the most anticipated party of the year.

Finally, we arrive at my office doors. I unlock the door, we step inside the empty room, and I don't let out the breath I've been holding until the door is locked behind me.

Lance Donner wastes no time, stepping up behind me and brushing his hands lightly against my hips as he leans close to my neck. Closing my eyes, I inhale, savoring the musky scent of his cologne.

Reopening my eyes, I bite my lip between my teeth as I examine the two men standing before me. I place a hand on each of their chests before taking a step back.

"So," I purr. "I think we all know why we're here. Yes?"

Lance Donner and Adam Vixen both nod in agreement, and I can sense their anticipation radiating from them.

My lips tilt upward. "Let's not waste any time, then."

Walking over to my desk, I pick up the bottle of champagne I stashed there earlier. Popping the cork, I pour each of us a glass of the bubbly liquid. They each take a glass, holding it firmly as they watch me, waiting for my orders.

I raise my glass to toast. "To all of us," I say, raising a brow. "To the promotions you are about to receive."

The three of us clink our glasses together, taking long, slow sips.

I set my glass down on the edge of my desk and walk toward the middle of the room. The two men follow me, stopping just behind me. I turn to face them, once again running my hands down their hard chests, feeling the warmth of their bodies through their button-up shirts.

"Let's take this night and make it a night to remember," I whisper, eyeing them up and down as I gauge their reactions while I slide the straps of my dress over my shoulders, letting it fall to the ground. I purposely wore *nothing* under my dress, and now I'm exposed and bare to the two of them. My heart races as I watch them stare back at me with the same desire in their eyes.

Lance Donner is the first to move, bringing his lips to mine and crashing into me with urgency. The heat of his body radiates against me as his strong hands caress my naked curves. I inhale deeply, sucking on his bottom lip as our kiss intensifies.

Then Adam Vixen's hands reach me, moving around my waist, pulling me from Lance's arms and into his. His lips trail down my neck, sending shivers down my spine. His tongue flicks against my skin, eliciting a low moan from my throat.

I can hear Lance undressing behind me, and I unzip Adam's pants, freeing his cock from the tight confinement of the expensive fabric. Adam groans as I take him in my hand, and he quickly unbuttons his shirt, leaving all three of us naked.

Their mouths and hands roam my body, exploring every inch of me with their tongues and fingers, and I feel lost in the moment.

This is what I've dreamed of from the moment I hired them.

Lance drops to his knees behind me, spreading my legs apart, exposing my pussy and my ass to his mouth. Gripping my ass cheeks firmly between his fingers, he parts them, giving him full access to my wet pussy. His hot tongue slides along my folds as he devours me, nipping and biting at my flesh.

While Lance is busy behind me, Adam is playing with my breasts, flicking his wet tongue over them and pinching my peaked nipples between his teeth. My back arches as I cry out, whimpering as the pleasure intensifies. Adam's hand travels down my stomach, then dips to my clit as Lance continues eating me from behind. Adam's fingers swirl around my clit, using both my arousal and Lance's spit to glide.

"Fuck yes," I moan, nearly collapsing as my knees shake.

Working Adam's cock in my hand, I lean forward, spreading myself wider for Lance while pulling Adam into my mouth. I slide my tongue along his shaft from base to tip, working slowly as he groans. He wraps his hands through my hair, controlling my head as I let him begin fucking my face.

Lance stands behind me, and I can feel his cock poking at my entrance. He slips inside me, dipping himself in shallow, then deeper and deeper with each deliciously wet thrust.

My head bobs up and down on Adam's cock while Lance fucks me from behind. Saliva falls from the sides of my mouth as Adam pumps himself in and out of me, sliding himself down my throat, then back out, occasionally stopping to slap the head of his dick on my face.

With hands firmly grasping my hips, Lance plows into me, pushing Adam's cock deeper down my throat. I gag and choke on his dick as Lance slams into me.

When I can't take anymore, I free my mouth of his dick, then say, "I want both of you inside of me."

Lance slows his pace, gently fucking me against his body as Adam lowers himself to the floor. Once Adam is flat on the floor, I climb on top of him, lining up his cock with my entrance, then sitting on it, letting it sink deep inside of me. I moan with pleasure as he fills me, and I bounce up and down a few times to adjust before Lance spits on my asshole, lubing it up as he pokes at my free hole. I lean forward, opening myself to him and giving him more space to join in.

Lance enters me an inch at a time, spitting the head of his dick each time he withdraws. Eventually, he's fully inside of me.

The two of them hold still as I begin to move, allowing my body time to adjust to having two massive cocks inside of me. Once I've picked up the pace, Lance begins pounding me from behind, gripping my hips as he fucks me. Adam laps at my nipples while I bounce and grind on his cock, angling myself just right so that my clit rubs against him.

I feel my orgasm building, starting in my toes as it works its way up. I feel lightheaded and euphoric as it blasts through me, and my hips fall into a rhythmic trance as I unravel.

Lance's hand comes down on my ass, the thunderous crack ringing through the air as he spanks me, and he picks up the pace.

My head falls back, and Lance grabs me by the throat while the two of them fuck me through my orgasm. I cry out, knowing I can be as loud as I want on this side of the office.

No one will hear us.

No one will catch us.

They're all intoxicated and slurring their words by now, but not me, no.

I'm sober as I ride Lance Donner and Adam Vixen. Their cocks fill me so much I feel like I'm going to burst, but it's so fucking good. I've worked my way into this powerful position in this corporate office, and now it's my turn to sit back and relax while everyone else tries to fuck their way to the top.

Lance Donner and Adam Vixen time their climaxes perfectly, both emptying themselves inside of me and filling me to the brim with their seed.

I smirk, smiling to myself.

It's exactly what I dreamed it would be.

On Donner, On Vixen.

About the Author

Dana LeeAnn is an author of dark romance, expanding into multiple sub-genres. She lives in northern Colorado with her husband and two kids. When not busy writing, you can find Dana spending time outdoors with her family or learning a new hobby.

Connect with Dana on social media:

Instagram: @danaleeannhunt

TikTok: @danaleeannhunt

Website for special editions and updates:

www.thedarkestromance.com

Facebook group:

https://www.facebook.com/groups/1266397124048561/

Acknowledgments

Thank you from the bottom of my heart.

To my **husband**, for being the best friend I could ever ask for, and for listening to me talk about the psychotically dark romance I love to not only read but think up. Your endless support gives me the confidence I need to keep going. This is for you, me, and our future. I love you.

To **Blake and Bailey**, for motivating me to be the best version of myself. I've found my dream, and I cannot wait for you to find yours. I'll be here every step of the way.

To **Giulia**, for designing the most incredible covers, and for making my visions come to life. Your creativity is so special. I will never take you for granted.

To my **betas and author friends** for always providing me with honest and sincere feedback. I am forever grateful!

To my **ARC readers**, for being the best hype team a girl could ask for. Your timely reviews make my life easier, and I can never thank you enough.

To my **readers**, for keeping me on my toes and giving me the best feedback. Sometimes criticism is hard, but I appreciate it more than you know.

Also by Dana LeeAnn

Carving for Cara (Wrecked Series #1)

Little Nightmare (Wrecked Series #2)

Crown of Blood and Stars (The Starling Series #1)

Lady of the Lost Fae (The Starling Series #2)

Season of Secrets

Made in the USA
Coppell, TX
06 November 2024